Downtown Green

Other books by Judy Christie

Gone to Green, book 1, The Green Series
Goodness Gracious Green, book 2, The Green Series
The Glory of Green, book 3, The Green Series
Rally 'Round Green, book 4, The Green Series

Hurry Less, Worry Less
Hurry Less, Worry Less at Christmas
Hurry Less, Worry Less at Work
Hurry Less, Worry Less for Families
Hurry Less, Worry Less for Moms

Awesome Altars (co-authored with Mary Dark)

Downtown Green

The Green Series

Judy Christie

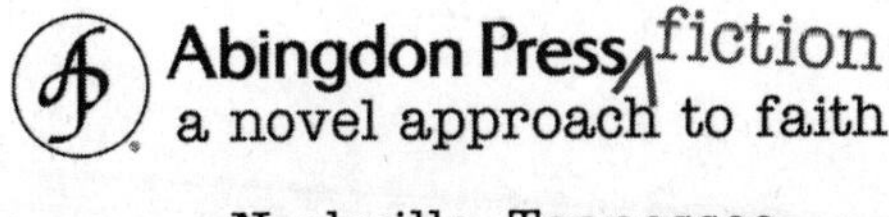

Nashville, Tennessee

Downtown Green

ISBN-13: 978-1-4267-0899-2

Published by Abingdon Press, P.O. Box 801, Nashville, TN 37202

www.abingdonpress.com

Published in association with the Books & Such Literary Agency, 5926 Sunhawk Drive, Santa Rosa, CA 95409, www.booksandsuch.biz

Library of Congress Cataloging-in-Publication Data

Christie, Judy Pace, 1956–
Downtown Green / Judy Christie.
p. cm. — (The Green series)
ISBN 978-1-4267-0899-2 (book - pbk. / trade pbk. : alk. paper) 1. Women journalists—Fiction. 2. Progress—Fiction. 3. City and town life—Louisiana—Fiction. 4. Communities—Louisiana—Fiction. 5. Community life—Louisiana—Fiction. I. Title.
PS3603.H7525D69 2012
813'.6—dc23

2011047286

Printed in the United States of America

1 2 3 4 5 6 7 8 9 10 / 17 16 15 14 13 12

To my Baylor Funfest Friends:
Annette Boyd, Mer Chaffin, Peggy Camerino,
Karen Enriquez, Ginger Hamilton, Laura Kimball,
Carol Lovelady, Laura Nolen, Gaye Slomka,
and Nancy Thompson

ACKNOWLEDGMENTS

Golden Pen Awards
from *The Green News-Item*
with Heartfelt Thanks from Lois Barker Craig
and Judy Christie

My gratitude has multiplied with each edition of *The Green News-Item* and every book in The Green Series. So many people encourage me and spread the word about Green. Thank you, all!

To the "reporters" who provide community news tidbits, Lois really should give you a raise. Special thanks to Carol Lovelady, Virginia Disotell, Ginger Hamilton, Mary Ann Van Osdell, Alan English, Martha Fitzgerald, Marilyn Rech, Eleanor Ransburg, Dot Ward, Dick Hooton, and Peggy Camerino.

Thanks, also, to Aunt Faye Kersh, Pat Lingenfelter, Kathie Rowell, Mary Frances Christie, Dr. Rob Weber, and my Grace Community United Methodist Church family; agents Etta Wilson and Janet Grant, who guide and coach; and the fantastic fiction team at Abingdon Press, including Ramona Richards, Julie Dowd, and editor Jenny Youngman.

And, always, love and thanks to my husband, Paul. Happy twentieth anniversary!

"Where's Iris?" Katy asked, stroking Ellie's arm lightly.

"She and Stan are coming later. They've moved back into the house down the road, and they're working on it. We're keeping an eye on Ellie."

The tiny girl's bottom lip trembled when I said her name. She stared right at me with bright blue eyes until I unbuckled her and lifted her out of the stroller.

"I knew you couldn't resist holding her," Tammy said. "Ellie's got Aunt Lois wrapped around her tiny little finger."

"She was unhappy," I said.

Tammy looked at Katy. "Lois grabs her if she so much as blinks. Eddie, too."

"You, on the other hand, wouldn't pick them up if they were screaming bloody murder." I adjusted the girl's insulated jumpsuit. "Do you think she's warm enough?"

Tammy snorted. "Since Iris has her dressed for the North Pole, she's probably burning up. Those poor kids have worrywarts for mothers."

"Being cautious doesn't make us worrywarts," I said, trying to recall a magazine article about overprotective moms. I was certain I'd filed it somewhere. "Kevin recommends infants stay bundled up during flu season."

"Flu season ended two weeks ago," Tammy said. "Fresh air is good for babies. My mother let me play outside in a diaper when I was that age."

"Look how you turned out," Katy said, grinning.

"Oh, Ellie's smiling," Molly said.

"That's gas," Tammy said.

A small nightlight glowed in the nursery when Chris and I went in to check on our son.

"Let's never tell Eddie he slept through his first party," I said as we stood by the cradle.

"At least he didn't cry," Chris said and leaned over and kissed the baby's soft cheek.

Looking around the sage green nursery, my eyes lingered on the lopsided quilt I'd made. The quilting group, started by my friend Kevin, included a mix of very different women. I enjoyed meeting with them to sew and visit, and their guidance had eased me into motherhood. My first quilt helped set the tone for the entire room, and the women had shown me the kind of mother I wanted to be.

Late at night, I loved to slip into the room and listen to my baby sleep. I would pull the old painted rocker close to his bed and snuggle under one of Estelle's afghans. Now, though, it was time to run through the bedtime checklist. "We've got the nightlight and baby monitor on," I said. "He's on his back, nothing near enough to smother him. He's not stopped up, so we don't need the humidifier. I wonder if it's too cool in here with the air-conditioning? Do you think we should move the cradle back into our room?"

"He's fine, Lois," Chris said. "You know we'll look in on him two dozen times before the night's over."

"But what if we don't hear him cry?"

"I'd say that's unlikely, since you check every two minutes to make sure the monitor's working."

"No, I don't," I said so loudly that Eddie jerked as he dozed. I smoothed his forehead and looked at Chris. "I do, don't I? I'm obsessed. I'm terrible! He'll need therapy to get over all my worrying." I wandered about the room, noting each item as a hazard in some way.

"You're not terrible," Chris said. "You're just a first-time mom."

"Tammy says Iris and I fret too much."

"That's what new parents do," he said. "You just add a certain layer of Lois to it. I'd expect nothing less."

"I love him so much," I said. "I can't believe I've lived this long without him in my life."

Chris nodded and rubbed Eddie's arm. The sight of my big, handsome husband gazing down at the little boy, who was drifting back to sleep, caused a wash of emotions so strong I couldn't put a name to them.

"Today was a great day, wasn't it?" I whispered.

"It sure was." Chris stepped back and draped his arm around my shoulder. "Eddie's first party. And you went back to the office."

"And?" I prompted.

"And Katy got home for spring break?" He had his irresistible teasing look on his face. That look, strong and gentle at the same time, made me feel like a character in a romance novel.

"*And?*" I said.

"And Mama said your banana pudding was better than hers?"

"*And?*"

He laughed softly and leaned over to kiss me. "And we celebrated two years of marriage."

"I thought maybe that had slipped your mind with all the commotion."

"Never." He put his forehead against mine for a moment. "I'll never forget the day I finally got you to be my wife."

I hugged him fiercely—thrilled, content, joyful. Then I pulled back and tiptoed over to the small closet, grabbing the present I'd stashed there before supper. "For you," I said.

He looked startled and tore into the package, whispering in delight when he saw the framed image of Eddie, "This is a great picture," he said.

"Tammy took it that Saturday she and Walt came by, right after Eddie was born," I said.

"How'd you have time to get this done?" he asked. "You've been so busy."

I felt rather smug. "I have my ways," I said and moved toward him.

Chris smiled and moved away, walking to the small chest of drawers we'd rescued from his parents' storage shed. Opening the top drawer, he reached under a stack of onesies and a large collection of light-blue and yellow outfits. He pulled out a wrapped gift very similar to the one he had just opened.

"Happy second anniversary," Chris said, kissing me thoroughly. My knees weak, I ripped the newspaper he had used for wrapping paper. Inside was the same black-and-white photo of Eddie that I had given Chris, in a slightly different frame.

"No wonder Tammy tried to talk me into a different shot," I said, keeping my laughter low.

"Great minds, right?" Chris said.

"Eddie sure is cute . . . and sweet," I said as we studied the identical photos of our new son. "Does everyone feel this way about their first baby?"

"Probably." Chris stroked my hair as he spoke.

"But Eddie is wonderful," I said.

"Absolutely. He's got Lois Barker Craig for a mom."

2

The Green Lawns Municipal Cemetery terminated its spring mowing crew after the employees "inappropriately and without thought" drove their lawn tractors to a local fast-food restaurant for soft drinks. "It's not like anybody died," the crew chief said, but the cemetery director disagreed.

—*The Green News-Item*

A dark blue sedan zipped around the orange cones that blocked the highway and whipped into the makeshift parking area, did a U-turn, and pulled to the shoulder near where we stood.

"What kind of idiot is that?" I asked, turning to see if Tammy had gotten a photograph for today's *News-Item.*

Mayor Eva added an annoyed huffing sound to my question. "I specifically directed the highway department not to let cars on until after the ceremony," she said, narrowing her eyes at the car. "People from D.C. think they can get away with anything."

"Are you sure that's the congressman?" I asked.

"Who else would come blazing down here like that?" she said, her eyes hidden behind a pair of huge sunglasses. She looked like a corporate CEO in her knit suit and with her brown hair styled in a bob. "They said he was running late, but that's no excuse for rude behavior."

"At least he didn't tear the ribbon," I said. A man in a business suit emerged from the car and walked toward us, his shiny shoes kicking up a cloud of dust.

My breath caught, and it wasn't from the dust.

In his late thirties, the man made the briefest eye contact with me, but extended his hand to businessman Dub McCuller. "Sorry for the delay, Mayor," he said in a Midwestern voice. "The congressman was delayed and asked me to give you his regards."

Dub didn't take his hand. "You've made a mistake, son," he said, tilting his head toward Eva. "Ms. Hillburn is the mayor, not me."

A flush ran up the familiar face. "I apologize, ma'am." He acknowledged Eva with a nod. "The congressman said to tell you, and I quote, 'I expect that highway to bring Green out of the Dark Ages.' "

"And you are . . . ?" Eva said. The last time I'd heard her use that tone was when her ex-husband tried to close Green's school. After three years in office, she'd perfected the official-function expression that now settled on her face.

"I'm Zach Price from Post Media Corp. Pleased to meet you." Zach flashed a big smile, and I expected to see sunlight sparkling off his teeth like in toothpaste commercials.

Eva pursed her lips, and Dub cocked his head even further. As for me, I froze, wishing among other things that I'd pressed my slacks and worn a dressier blouse.

"If we weren't already behind schedule, I'd try to discern why you're here, but . . ." Eva looked at her watch again. "You can fill me in later on why our good congressman stood me up."

With the mayor leading the way to the center of a makeshift platform, Zach edged his way in front of Dub and me, and said something to Eva in a soft voice. She nodded.

Tammy, camera in hand, strode over, a curious look on her face. "Who is that guy?" she hissed into my ear. "He's cute, but he acts like a jerk."

Shaking my head, I said nothing, still following Eva and trying to decide what would be appropriate to say. My heart thudded as I pushed closer to the journalist.

Before I could catch his attention, the roar of another car engine drowned out my words. A souped-up classic car, painted bright blue, zoomed up Route Two and swerved onto the brand-new entrance ramp. It burst through the ribbon stretched across the road and caused VIPs to jump out of the way.

"So much for the grand opening," Zach said in an I'm-in-charge voice. "What was that all about?"

The driver of the old car waved as the vehicle disappeared from view. A buzz, somewhat agitated, somewhat excited, ran through the small crowd. People shook their heads and frowned.

However, it wasn't the bright-colored hotrod that had scrambled my thoughts. Following the mayor to the huddle of visiting politicians and road bureaucrats, I was thinking about Zach.

"Is everyone OK? No injuries?" Eva asked those gathered around her.

"Nothing hurt except the ribbon," a Bouef Parish police juror said, holding up the ripped red fabric.

"A minor detail," Eva said, her demeanor calm. *How did she do that?* I had once seen her knock a glass of water off a lectern during a speech and never miss a word. Today was no different. "Ladies and gentlemen, prepare to start your engines," she yelled to the crowd. Even when yelling, she managed to sound in control. "Our official program begins in five minutes."

A smattering of applause from the crowd of government officials and a few businesspeople in Green followed her words, and people went back to visiting. The attendees were almost one-hundred-percent supporters of the highway. Noticeably absent were those who insisted the bypass would be the end of downtown Green.

From nearly the moment I had first driven into town, I knew the road was coming, one way or the other. I hadn't allowed myself to embrace it, but I tried to be optimistic.

The mayor outlined the upcoming program to those surrounding her and introduced assorted bureaucrats and politicians to Zach as though they were heads of state. She worked her way down the line to me. "Lois, I believe you've met Zach Price, news executive from Post Media," she said. "I understand you two worked together in Dayton."

"Lois Barker," Zach said, reaching in to hug me as I held out my hand, creating an awkward half-hug.

"Craig," I said. "Lois Craig."

"Oh, that's right," he said. "I heard you got married and are going to have a baby." His eyes lingered on my stomach for a moment.

"I had a baby on New Year's Day," I said with a smile that I hoped reflected how contented I was.

"Cute, cute, cute," Eva said. "That baby's a doll." Then she excused herself to speak to a state senator from Natchitoches.

Assuming my newspaper-owner persona, I tilted my head. "What are you doing here, Zach?" Seeing him in Green was like seeing a famous TV weatherman in your neighborhood. It couldn't be good news.

"I'm touring the state," Zach said, "familiarizing myself with Louisiana."

"Why do you need to learn about Louisiana?" I asked. "It's not exactly a corporate hub."

"You never know."

"What's that supposed to mean?" I had hated his smirks in Dayton, and they looked even worse than I remembered in the bright sunshine. The bright sunshine of *my* turf.

"Post News has been given a substantial journalism grant to come up with news coverage in small communities. They've asked me to get things rolling."

"But Green has news coverage," I said.

"We're exploring efficient, innovative ways to consolidate coverage with fewer resources," Zach said. He pulled a small thread off his sleeve and flicked it away. "The entire news platform has shifted since you left the business."

"I didn't leave the business," I said, and, for good measure, I flicked my own piece of lint off my shirt.

"Oh, that's right," he said. "You manage the little news operation here in Green."

"I own the newspaper."

"The local weekly. I remember." He nodded as he spoke, his tone arrogant.

"Twice weekly," I snapped. "The *News-Item* has been named one of the best small newspapers in the country."

"Twice weekly, oh, yeah." He dismissed my paper with his chuckle.

"The *Item* also has a solid web presence," I said, "and is making money when many newspapers are not."

His expression shifted, the way it used to when a news story caught his attention in Dayton. "So I hear," he said. "I believe you're going to like the grant partnership. Louisiana has been ignored far too long. Post Media sees lots of potential in this region. They've asked me to establish a presence here."

"You're staying?" I blurted the question. He might as well have told me he was being transferred to a remote village on another continent.

"You don't keep up with the newspaper grapevine, do you?" he said. "The new highway opens possibilities for collaboration with Southern newspapers. We want to create a model for all our papers. We'll set up regional offices and work with local municipalities."

A ladybug landed on his sleeve, and he brushed it off. "A highway like this one changes everything," he said. "More industry is possible. Small towns like Green aren't cut off the way they once were."

I hated the way he emphasized my town's name, making it sound like an infectious disease. "Green hasn't been cut off," I said. "It's a great place to live."

"Maybe it used to be," he said, "but I've looked at the stats. Unemployment's high, test scores are low, and there's not one manufacturer. The new industrial park near downtown will be a boon to the economy."

"The industrial park is only one option," I said. "The Green Forward Group has many opportunities to consider."

Before he could respond, another car zoomed up on the bypass.

"What's with these people?" Zach demanded.

Incredulous, I glared at the car and back at him. "You did the same thing."

"That was different," he said.

Gravel flew from under the tires of the car as it whirled into the parking area. "Don't start without me, Lois," Katy yelled out the window as she looked for a spot to park, a fluorescent bumper sticker advertising the university she attended.

"You know her?" Zach asked.

"She's a reporter for the *Item,*" I said, briefly smiling despite my annoyance at Katy's tardy arrival.

Katy rushed up. "Cutting it a little close, aren't you?" I asked.

"I'm sorry, Lois. I know I wasn't supposed to drive on the road, but it's finished, and it's so much quicker. I overslept. I was in a hurry."

"I noticed."

"So you're a reporter?" Zach jumped in, and I wondered if it was journalistic interest or male delight that brought his flirtatious grin.

"Broadcast major," Katy said with the careless confidence she wore so well at age nineteen. "And I blog."

Reaching inside his jacket, Zach pulled out a small leather card case and handed a business card to Katy, one of my handful of staff members. "Zach Price, Post Media, former colleague of Lois's," he said. "We recruit students around the country for our young-reader initiative, if you're interested."

"Wait a minute!" I exclaimed. "Katy works for me."

"Forever?" Zach asked, in the tone he used when he was my boss. "Or for now?"

Katy looked from me to Zach with her brow furrowed. "I thought Lois said you worked up North somewhere," she said.

"I'm in the Post corporate offices in Omaha," he said.

"What are you doing in Green?" she asked. Ahh, how I loved Katy.

"We're starting a pilot program for small-town coverage," he said. I'd seen that look on his face enough to know that I'd better listen closely. "North Louisiana is one of the sites under consideration, depending on what happens downtown."

"Does that mean you might open an office here?" Katy directed the question at him but cut her eyes in my direction.

"My, you *are* a reporter, aren't you?" Zach said. "I definitely want to hire you."

"Lois?" Katy said. "What's going on? Is this guy trying to take over the paper?"

"You're *good.*" Zach managed to gush and preen in the same breath.

I tried to mask my dismay at Zach's words, and exhaled in relief when Eva interrupted the conversation.

Holding a cheerleader's megaphone painted by a Green High art class, the mayor called for everyone's attention. "Look at this," she said, somehow managing to sweep one arm toward the new road without losing her grip on her sound system. "Two years ago, a tornado tried to blow us away," she said. "We have worked hard to recover. Today, stronger than ever, we drive into the future of Green."

A ripple of applause ran through the crowd on the beautiful spring day. The bright white of Bradford pear trees glowed in the one yard left nearby.

"People talk about the death of little towns," Eva said. "They say bypasses like this one can cut out the heart of a place. But they don't know Green, do they?" She punctuated her comments with a wave of her hand.

"You're right about that," the hardware store owner yelled.

"We're strong!" Marcus Taylor, head of the Lakeside Neighborhood Association and my best friend's father, shouted.

"Amen!" Jean, my pastor from Grace Chapel, added.

The crowd clapped more.

"We've had our challenges in Green," Eva continued. "No one denies that. Nevertheless, we refuse to board up downtown and watch it fade away. This splendid new highway will work with—not against—our plans for downtown."

I swallowed hard at the word *plans,* not sure that we actually had any.

"And now Lois Barker Craig, newspaper owner and president of the Green Forward Group, will say a few words." Eva touched me on the shoulder as she took a seat next to Dub.

Zach's mouth twisted ever so slightly as I slipped past him to hoist the megaphone.

"What an amazing day," I said. "Isn't this something?" I paused, soaking up the emotion of the moment. It was a beautiful spring day in North Louisiana, and Chris and I had married on almost this very spot.

"We lost some very special things in the tornado," I said and nodded toward where the little Grace Community Chapel had once sat. "And some incredible people." A hush came over the crowd when my voice broke. "But new life has sprung forth. We choose to see possibilities, instead of problems. To look ahead, instead of behind."

Tammy let loose with one of her famous whistles.

"You tell 'em, Lois," Katy yelled. Perhaps I should talk to my staff about their objectivity. I glanced at Zach, who had a disapproving look on his face.

Or maybe I shouldn't.

That kind of enthusiasm would help us figure out how to keep Green alive.

Mornings with a new baby were so chaotic that I made up headlines to suit them.

"Dog Goes Berserk in SUV," I said when I put an excited Holly Beth in her crate in the back of the used vehicle. We had traded my small car the week before Eddie was born.

"Car Seats Not Friendly to Harried Mom," I imagined when I fastened Eddie into his car seat and headed to work.

"Time Management an Art Form for New Mothers," I mumbled when, hardly out of the driveway, I realized I'd forgotten my green leather tote. I was nearly to Iris Jo's old house when I remembered the diaper bag.

"Newspaper Owner Fondly Recalls Breakfast," I thought when my stomach growled, Eddie wailing and in need of an emergency diaper change and Holly Beth whining as though deserted in a cage in the jungle.

By the time I rolled up to the sign where Route Two approached the new highway, twenty minutes late for a conference call with the *Item's* newsprint supplier, I passed my usual turn and drove up the smooth new ramp onto the bypass.

I had stuck with my old path since the road opened two weeks earlier, enjoying familiar yards in springtime and stubbornly not giving in to the new highway that had the town in an uproar. It wouldn't hurt to use the new route once.

Exiting just beyond downtown, I doubled back and made it to the newspaper in record time. I paused on the steps to read the painted names of those who had died since yesterday's edition, one of my favorite *News-Item* traditions. I shifted Eddie's carrier and tried to control Holly Beth.

"So, what'd you think?" Tammy asked, holding the door open and raising her eyebrows.

I looked at the names again. "No surprises," I said.

"Not about the obituaries," she said. "The bypass."

"How'd you know I came that way?"

"You turned into the parking lot from a different direction." She grinned, petting my dog and ignoring my son. "I've wondered how long it would take you to start using it. Saved you fifteen minutes, didn't it?"

"I'm not going to make a habit of it," I said. "I like my regular route better, but I was running behind today."

Placing the baby carrier on the counter, I let the dog off her leash and collected the out-of-town papers, tote bag, and a half a cup of cold coffee.

Eddie's quilt, a gift from the quilting group, got stuck in the lobby's swinging door as I made my way to my office, and I heard a small rip as I yanked it.

I inhaled. Exhaled. Inhaled.

"Rough morning?" Tammy asked.

"It used to be so easy to get out of the car and to my desk," I said.

"You're not complaining about Eddie, are you?"

"Of course not," I said. "I just feel disorganized."

"You're so lucky," she said and gave Holly Beth another pat before she went back to her desk.

Within a week, my vehicle automatically veered onto the bypass, and I saw with fresh eyes why some residents thought it was affecting Green's businesses.

"Eddie woke us up ten times last night," I said when Tammy commented on my new travel pattern the next day.

"I stopped to check on Chris's parents," I said another day.

"I had to run an errand," I said at the end of the next week.

Tammy rolled her eyes, and I gave up. "It's just so much quicker than I expected," I said.

"Told you so," she replied.

3

If you have a good propane grill to spare, members of the Amos Cutoff Praise Church need it. "Our grill blew up during our regular Sunday night meal," one of my neighbors said. "Meat and potatoes wrapped in foil flew all over the place. Our preacher said he thought for a minute it was our last supper before we met in heaven."

—The Green News-Item

My loving husband shooed me out of the house on a Saturday afternoon near the middle of May.

"Eddie and I have some baseball to watch," Chris said when we got home from our weekly breakfast with his parents. "Do something fun for a change. Let me watch our boy for a while."

"Really?" I asked, the thought of leaving Eddie both appalling and appealing.

"Your mommy thinks I can't handle you, little man," Chris teased, cradling Eddie like a football. "She doesn't realize that the locker room at school smells way worse than anything you can dish out."

"When you put it like that . . . ," I said.

"Haven't I turned into a good diaper changer?" he asked.

"The best."

"Then get out of here. Take Holly Beth for a drive or something."

"You know what I'd really like to do?" I asked.

"I'm guessing it has something to do with that newspaper you run."

"On the nose," I said, leaning in to kiss Eddie's cute little nose. "I want to clean off my desk. It looks worse than our laundry room."

"That's not the kind of fun I had in mind," Chris protested. "Go to the Holey Moley or go see Kevin or something."

"Cleaning off my desk will be fun," I said. "There's no telling what I'll discover in that rat's nest."

Chris lowered his head to Eddie's ear. "I hate to break it to you, pal, but your mom's wound tight," he murmured. "That means she gets lots of stuff done."

Laughing, I kissed the men in my life and picked up Holly Beth's leash. The moment she saw me do that, she ran to the back door and gave one sharp bark. As I hoisted her into the front seat of the SUV, she looked at me, then looked back at the house and whined.

"I can't tell if you're happy or sad that we're leaving Eddie today," I said, "but it's just us girls now."

She yelped as though she understood every word and wagged her tail furiously. I had indeed turned into one of those people who talk to dogs as if they're human.

"Hmmm," I said, lighthearted all of a sudden. "I do believe you're happy to have me all to yourself."

Downtown was empty when I pulled onto Main Street, and I felt disoriented. Between the vacant street and leaving Eddie at home, it seemed as if I had forgotten something or gotten my days mixed up.

After parking in the *Item's* small lot, I put Holly Beth on her leash and headed up the steps. My hair in a ponytail, the late spring sun felt good on my neck, and I sat down on the steps, my legs stretched out. Holly Beth climbed into my lap, and I snuggled her for a moment.

"Right here on this very spot is where I got you," I said in the baby voice I also used with Eddie. "Mayor Eva handed you over to me, and you weren't any bigger than my hand."

Holly licked my face and jumped down, dragging her leash. Her friskiness and the sunshine made the pile of paperwork inside seem less urgent.

"You're ready for a walk, aren't you, girl?" I asked and glanced around to make sure no one was listening. Not a dog person until I had encountered Chris and his three mutts, I was still amazed at how much I enjoyed each of our pets.

"You win," I said, grabbing the leash. Holly's tail wagged furiously, and she gave me a look almost like a smile. Walking to the sidewalk, I looked to the right, the left, and the right again, stunned at how quiet it was. It reminded me of the New Year's Day when I had first come to Green. That day only Katy had been in sight.

Now, a flash of orange down the block caught my eye, and I officially abandoned my plans to clean off my desk, happy to see Becca waving from her flower shop.With her standard wicker basket in one hand and a watering can in the other, she wore khaki Capri pants topped off by a short-sleeved blouse and looked more like a college student than an up-and-coming entrepreneur.

"I hope you've come to buy flowers," she said when I drew near. "I've ordered more than I need."

"Slow day?" I asked, trying to keep Holly from jumping on her.

"More like a slow year," she said, kneeling to pet the dog. "Look around."

Scanning the other businesses, including the Antique Mall, Mayor Eva's department store, and the pharmacy, I looked for a hint of a customer. Even Rose's truck was missing at the Holey Moley Antique Mall. "I haven't seen it this dead since the tornado," I said. "Is something going on south of town?"

"Nothing's going on anywhere in Green," Becca said, watering the window boxes on the front of her store. "People don't cut through town anymore, and folks are going to Shreveport instead of shopping here. I'm scared, Lois."

I already used Eddie's age as the starting point for time in my life, and I counted backwards to figure out how many weeks had passed since the grand opening of the highway.

"Surely the road can't have had this much impact in two months."

"It's like that weed on the lake," she said. "It got bad quick. "Even my warehouse guy folded." Becca set the watering container next to a potted gardenia and drew the small clippers out of her basket. "He couldn't match the prices at the chain stores in Shreveport. He sent an email last week asking if anyone knew of any job openings."

She snipped brown leaves from the fern and stashed them in her basket. "Two restaurants have closed, too," she said. "Their supper business shriveled up."

"I know," I said with a sigh. "They were decent advertisers, too. We've written several stories, but seeing it like this . . . I didn't realize things were quite so bad. I'm surprised Eva hasn't come by to talk about it."

A strained look took over Becca's face, the shade from the store making her look grim. "The mayor's out of town. She announced it at our last downtown meeting."

I sorted through my mental calendar but couldn't think of much that didn't revolve around Eddie. "I may have missed that meeting," I said.

"Eva went to a conference for city officials in Orlando two weeks ago."

"She's been gone for two weeks? That doesn't sound like her." It didn't sound like me either not to know where the mayor was. "I can't see her leaving town for that long."

Becca hesitated. "This is gossip, but I heard that Dub flew down there with her, and he and the mayor went on a vacation after the meeting. That's caused raised eyebrows among the few customers I have left. People say she should be here, trying to save the town, not flitting around with a criminal."

"Ex-criminal," I said, unable to keep the indignation out of my voice. "Dub's done a lot to clear his good name, and Eva's more committed to Green than anyone I know."

"Apparently people aren't ready to forgive Dub's past along with this slide in business." Becca paused again. "They're saying Eva's not herself since that mess with the schools and that shifty consultant."

I jerked Holly's leash a little harder than I intended and tapped at the dirt in the window box, where a small root poked out. "Fighting to keep the school open was hard on Eva," I said. "She had no idea her husband—ex-husband, that is—would try to shut the schools down. She hadn't seen him in years."

"I like the mayor," Becca said, "but I see where people are coming from. My business isn't going to make it without leadership. Two days this week I didn't sell one single thing, not even a greeting card."

She rubbed at a smudge on her display window with a white cloth. "I know you've got a lot on your hands with Eddie and your remodeling project . . ." Her voice trailed off, and I didn't know what to say. "What do you think we should do?" she finished in a rush.

"The mayor's private business is her business," I said. "We should let her and Dub sort it out."

"I didn't mean what should we do about the mayor's love life," she said, an unfamiliar sign of exasperation on her face. "How can we stop this downtown trend? Saturdays used to be my busiest day. I won't last with many more weekends like this one."

"We'll come up with something," I said, wanting to sound more energetic than I felt. When people talked about the future of downtown, they were talking about the future of my beloved *Green News-Item.* All I could think of at this moment was how Eddie and Chris were getting along without me.

"You have the best ideas, Lois," Becca said. "We need something like the Fall Festival or the Christmas project, except all year. I don't want Green to disappear."

Becca looked so earnest and her compliment sounded so sincere that I didn't have the heart to walk away. "Maybe together we can come up with something," I said, looking at my watch.

Holly Beth pulled at her leash and barked. "Any chance you have time for a walk?" I asked. "We could head toward the lake and see how things look."

"Why not?" Becca replied. "It's not like I'm going to miss a customer." She stuck a hand-lettered sign on the door. "Back soon. Becca," it read. Then she adjusted the plastic hands on a sign with a clock on it.

"I had to let my helper go," she said.

My own staff popped into my mind. We were sparse as it was. What if I had to lay someone off?

My lighthearted feeling had dissolved, and I looked at the newspaper as we headed toward the lake. Holly danced around ahead of us, investigating each crack in the sidewalk and peeing on an old-fashioned light post. The green azalea bushes, not a bloom left, reminded me how fast spring in North Louisiana passes and summer settles in.

Becca pointed at Holly Beth. "At least she's in a good mood."

"She likes my attention," I said, bending over to pat Holly's fur. "She's not quite used to Eddie."

"We went through the same thing when my daughter was born," Becca said. "Our dog did not like Cassie one bit, but now they're best buddies."

My head bobbed in surprise. "I had no idea you had a little girl."

"With everything that's happened since I bought the shop, you and I haven't gotten to know each other very well," Becca said without the snippiness the sentence could have held. "I spend most of my time holed up in my workroom, and you're on the run with your son and the paper."

"I don't like being so busy," I said. "It's frustrating."

She made a sympathetic noise. "It's what all moms do, right?"

"So it seems," I said. "I never realized quite how tough it would be . . . tough and wonderful."

"Having a baby changes everything," she said. Even though Eddie was an infant, I already could recognize the look in her eyes, the soft look a mother gets when she thinks about her child.

"Is it hard for you?" I asked. "Being a mother? Because other women make it look easy."

"It's like a pop quiz every day," she said.

"Exactly!" I relaxed with the admission. "Half the time I pray I don't do any lasting damage to Eddie. Babies are so perfect . . ." I tried to think of how to describe Eddie—and Ellie, who felt like part of my family. "They're precious."

Becca smiled and nodded knowingly.

"What's your daughter's name?" I asked.

"Cassie. She turned four on January 1. She's a New Year's baby."

"So is Eddie! I rang in the year in labor at the lovely Green Medical Center."

"I've never met anyone else who had a baby on January 1," she said. "It's kind of weird, isn't it?"

"Especially since Chris's family, my staff, and half the members of Grace Chapel were whooping it up in the waiting room," I said. "If Kevin hadn't been my doctor, we'd have gotten kicked out before Eddie ever came."

"Dr. Kevin Taylor? Her mother comes in the shop sometimes. She's such a nice lady."

"Pearl and Marcus are great people, and Kevin's my best friend in Green," I said. "She's amazing. The first African American doctor in town, renovates houses for poor people, you name it. And she was right there for the party when my son was born."

"Things were quieter when Cass was born," Becca said. "My mother drove me to the hospital, but she had to get home to check on my brother. He can't stay by himself."

"Is he ill?" I ran through my mind for a clue about Becca's family, but couldn't remember much other than that she lived in the Ashland community.

"He had a motorcycle accident, and he's been in a wheelchair for a few years."

I murmured an awkward word of condolence. "What about Cassie's father?" I asked. "Is he shy like you?"

The other woman sped up her pace. "He's not involved in Cassie's life," she said. "We sort of went about things in the wrong way."

An image of Chris and me standing together by Eddie's crib at night came to my mind, and I felt a pang of sadness for Becca. "You're stronger than I am," I said. "I was such a big baby that Chris had to hold my hand. If he left, I started yelling." I twisted my mouth at the memory. "It was not my finest hour. I can't imagine doing this mom thing without Chris. I'd be even more scattered than I am now." I smiled and hoped my remarks sounded like a compliment and not criticism.

"I'm babbling," I said. "That's what I do these days. I babble." I looked over at her. "How do you stay so put together?"

"First, Cassie's older. I've had more time to practice," Becca said. "My mother's a big help, too. She's taken care of my brother since he was in the wreck, and she's so good to me and Cassie."

"You're fortunate to have your mom," I said. I'd missed my mother so much since Eddie's birth.

"I have a wonderful grandmother, too. She lives out by the new bypass in the house with the uprooted trees in the front yard," Becca added.

I could picture the house, and felt my familiar dismay at how the corner had changed.

"We want Gran to move in with us, but she refuses. They bulldozed half her lawn, but she says she's staying until she goes across the road to the cemetery."

"I couldn't leave Route Two either," I said.

"This area gets in your blood, doesn't it?"

"Something got in my blood," I said with a laugh. "Next thing I know, I'm married and have a son in Green, Louisiana. How about you?"

"I grew up in Ashland," she said. "Your wedding was one of my first big jobs at the flower shop. I've never really thanked you properly for giving me that chance."

"You did a wonderful job," I said. "It looked like a garden, exactly the way I wanted. Goodness! Cassie must have been hardly more than a baby when you took over the shop. That took a lot of courage."

"Most days I thought I had taken leave of my senses," Becca said, "but I needed a way to make money, and there weren't any jobs. It was a risk I needed to take."

"I can't imagine trying to do that with Eddie."

"You run the town," she said with a mild, scolding tone. "Your work is way more challenging than mine. People come to me for corsages; they come to you for leadership."

"You're giving me too much credit," I said, gesturing. "Katy says I'm bossy, and Tammy calls me a know-it-all."

She laughed, and we were silent for a moment. I held my face up to the sun, like a turtle on a log in Chris's catfish ponds. "It feels good, doesn't it?" I said.

She tilted her face likewise. "It certainly does. I needed this visit today."

"Me, too," I said, but my heart sank as I got a good look at Bayou Lake.

"Oh, my," Becca said.

Silently we stood side by side in the park that once featured a lovely view of water. Now it was all weeds. "Winter didn't kill it," I said. "The herbicides they've sprayed haven't. They're even talking about releasing some sort of weevil to eat it."

"Couldn't that bug create a new problem?" Becca asked. "No one could have known when they brought this plant to Louisiana that it would do this."

"The same thoughts go 'round and 'round in my mind," I said. "Maybe the only real option *is* to drain the lake."

"I suppose that could pay off later," she said. "It'll sure hurt us now, though."

"I'm not very patient." I attempted a laugh. "I want a quick fix."

She shook her head slowly. "I've found there aren't many quick fixes."

My spirits drooped more. "We'd better be getting back," I said. "Eddie's probably finished the bottles I left, and Chris needs to meet with his coaching volunteers."

As we strolled toward the paper, Holly Beth tugged hard on her leash and broke free, running full speed toward a crew of workers unloading a bulldozer between the Methodist church and the abandoned ice-cream stand.

"Holly Beth, stay!" I shouted.

"What are they doing?" Becca gasped.

Looking beyond my dog, I saw two men stapling yellow caution tape on posts around the lot and building. One of them was the contractor on our house project. The other was Lee Hicks, my one-time adversary at the paper.

"Lee!" I yelled, just as my dog jumped on his legs.

Becca had charged forward at the first sight of the workers, but stopped, her face the gray-white color of the pavement. "Who is that?" she asked, tugging on my arm.

"That's our builder," I said. "He runs his father's business."

She shook her head wildly. "The other guy," she said, pointing to the man with Holly Beth.

"That's Lee," I said. "He's a carpenter."

Becca seemed to examine Lee and took a step backward. "He's not Lee Roy Hicks, the guy who used to work at the paper?" Her voice sounded choked.

"It's Lee Hicks. He dropped the 'Roy' after prison." I laughed when I realized how weird that sounded. "He's changed a lot in the last three years. He lives in a travel trailer in our yard, which even I find hard to believe."

As I spoke, Holly Beth hurled herself at Lee again. Holly Beth liked me and adored Chris, but she idolized Lee. He'd kept her for a few days when Eddie was born, and I suspected she was wounded that she had had to move back in with us.

"Hey, sweet pea," Lee said, picking Holly up and ruffling her fur when we approached. "How's the best dog in town?"

Wearing paint-stained jeans with a rip at the knee and an old Green High T-shirt, he looked different from his days as business manager at the *News-Item.* Then he'd been pressed, starched, and spotless. Moreover, the kindness in his eyes was far different from in those days.

The sun glinted in his thick gold hair, and he looked like someone who trained at the gym instead of a carpenter whose paychecks had repaid the paper for theft.

"Lois, where's the little guy?" Lee asked when he'd finished babying Holly Beth. He looked over my shoulder, clearly searching for Eddie.

"Mom's day out," I said. "Becca and I are taking a walk, talking about the future of downtown." I inclined my head toward the florist.

"Becca?" Lee's head jerked at the sound of the name.

"Hello, Lee Roy," she said, the slightest hint of a tremble in her soft voice.

"It's Lee," I said, embarrassed. "He goes by Lee now."

"Oh, right." Becca's words were stronger now. "I forgot. He's changed."

"I don't believe I've bumped into you since I've been out of jail," he said, his voice softening. "You look good. How's your mother?"

"You two know each other?" I asked. Lee hesitated, glancing at Becca.

"Lee Roy and my brother were friends years ago," she said. "Lois, don't you need to get back?"

I made a big show of looking at my watch, even though I knew exactly what time it was. "I do, but first I want to hear what's going on here."

Becca put her hand up like a stop sign. "Nothing's going on. I need to reopen my shop."

I looked back at the bulldozer near the ice cream stand. "Something's going on. There's a piece of machinery sitting there and yellow tape everywhere."

Becca and Lee exhaled at the same moment. "Oh, the building project," Lee said.

"What did you think I was talking about?" I said. The man and woman looked at each other, Lee taking a step toward Becca, and Becca taking a step away.

"We're getting ready to tear that old building down," Lee said. "It's a shame, isn't it?"

"Tear it down?" Becca's voice was back to normal. "Who would do something like that?"

Lee looked uncomfortable. "You'll have to ask my boss about that. I'm not involved in the business end of things." He picked up a sledgehammer. "I'm on the tell-me-what-to-do end of things."

"That's a classic Southern drive-in. There are very few still intact and hardly any with a water view," Becca said. "How can you even think of bulldozing that? It's the best building in Green."

The sentence was by far the longest thing I'd ever heard her say, and I apparently wasn't the only one taken aback by her pronouncement.

"Are you an architect now?" Lee asked.

"I have a flower and gift shop, but I've been researching small-town development," she said. "This building is a treasure."

"Becca owns Blossoms and Gifts," I said.

"Wow, congratulations," Lee said. "You always dreamed of your own business, but no one told me you'd done it."

I felt like I'd come in during the middle of a soap opera I hadn't seen for a while. I vaguely recognized the characters but couldn't follow the story line.

"I did," Becca said, scuffing her foot on the sidewalk.

"So, what's happening here? What's the real story on that building?"

Lee's brow furrowed. "We were hired to prepare the site for a teardown."

"Why?" I asked.

"When?" Becca asked.

"Like I said, you need to talk to the boss about that," he said. "Major Wilson's involved. Everyone knows you two don't get along, Lois."

"I get along with him fine now that he's in jail."

"Uh . . ." Lee said.

"I've tried to think better of him since he loaned us that camper," I interrupted. "Lee stays there now, Becca, at least until our house is one-hundred-percent finished."

"Umm," Lee said again. He took a deep breath, the uneasy look on his face intensifying.

"Is something wrong?" I asked.

"I suppose it's public record what Major's doing," Lee said. "He plans to sell this lot to a developer. If this deal goes through, he's going to do the same with those buildings over there." He nodded to a row of storefronts across the street.

"He's promoting it on his website as the perfect place for the industrial park," Lee continued.

"His website?" My laugh sounded a bit like a cackle, even to my own ears. "He can't do that kind of business from jail."

Lee glanced quickly at Becca, then looked at Holly, who rested across one of his work boots.

"I thought you of all people would have heard," he said, finally looking at me. "Major got out of jail a few days ago."

4

Ruby Barnhill has magnolia blossoms for anyone who wants them. "They don't last long, but they smell so good," she said. The eighty-seven-year-old widow chopped her prize magnolia tree down after the power company trimmed the top out of it. "I couldn't bear the way they butchered it, so I got out Jim's old chainsaw and cut it down. I'm going to miss that tree."

—The Green News-Item

Katy pulled into our driveway at break-neck speed, then slammed on the brakes and glanced down at her cell phone at the same time. Molly sat in the passenger's seat, apparently reading a book.

"When did Katy get such a lead foot?" Chris asked, Eddie lying stretched out on his legs in the porch swing, the late May evening the perfect temperature.

"One of many things she's picked up at college," I said. "She seemed at loose ends during spring break. I'm hoping she'll settle down a little during her internship in New York."

"Katy's always at loose ends," Chris said as the girls got out of the car.

"No, she's not. She's matured during the last couple of years. She's just restless."

"I guess we were all restless at that age," he said.

"Guess who's out for the summer?" Katy said, swooping right past me to Eddie, giving one of her trademark squeals.

"Hey, Lois, Coach," Molly said, walking up with her, shaking her head, a sociology textbook in hand. "She couldn't wait to see Eddie. She just got in."

As if on cue, my son started what his grandma called squalling, which sounded like out-and-out screaming to me. Between Katy's shrieks and Eddie's tears, the noise was earsplitting, and all four dogs started barking loudly and running around the backyard as though their tails were on fire.

"Shhhh, quiet down," I said, not sure whether I was addressing Katy, the dogs, or Eddie.

"Oh, Lois, he's perfect, perfect, perfect," Katy squealed again. "He's even cuter than I remembered. Can I hold him? Molly, isn't he adorable?"

My head spun with Katy's exuberance, but Molly, Katy's best friend and a college student, convenience store clerk, and my part-time newspaper employee, smiled tolerantly.

"He is precious," Molly said, stroking Eddie's head.

Chris shifted in the swing to make room for Katy and started to hand her the baby.

"Wait!" I said so sharply that the dogs barked again. "You've got to wash your hands first."

"Oh, sure," Katy said.

"Follow me, and you can see all we've done since you were home," I said. "Molly, you haven't seen my latest painting project either." As we walked into the house, I heard Chris talking quietly to Eddie. I thought I caught the words *girls*, *squealing*, and *trouble*, but I wasn't sure.

With the pride of an interior designer, I herded the two into Eddie's room, where I had painted a huge tree on one of the walls.

"I didn't know you were artistic," Katy said.

"I'm not," I said. "Becca sketched it and told me what kind of paint to use."

"Show Katy what you've done to the porch," Molly said. "It's my favorite part of the house."

"Mine, too," I said, thinking of evenings when Chris and I took time to sprawl on the huge screened back porch, Eddie playing on his quilt on the painted concrete floor.

Katy squealed again as she stepped out onto the porch, and I jumped. "Is she getting louder, or am I getting crankier?" I asked Molly.

"Probably a little of both," Molly said, punching her friend lightly in the arm.

"I love this, I love this, I love this," Katy said, flopping down on the single bed suspended by ropes from the ceiling. A quilt, made by Chris's grandmother as a young bride, covered the mattress.

Molly smiled, looking around at the big woven rugs, a cluster of rockers and gliders, ceiling fans, and the wood-burning stove in the corner. I added my smile, enjoying the presence of my favorite young women in our home.

"Chris saw that bed in a magazine and surprised me with it," I said. "It arrived last week."

"I could spend my whole summer right here," Katy swooned. "Try it out, Molly. Try it out." She patted the cushion, and her friend flopped down beside her.

"This feels like old times," I said, "having you both here. I wish you didn't have to leave again for New York."

Katy stood up so fast that the hanging bed swung wildly.

"My internship fell through," she said with the slightest hesitation.

"Fell through? But you're one of their summer regulars. They love you up there."

"I kind of, well, sort of . . ." Katy stalled. "I declined the internship. I want to work at the *Item* full-time."

"Won't it be the best to have Katy around again?" Molly jumped in, always lieutenant and defender for Katy.

"I love having both of you around, but what happened to 'I'm a big city girl, and I'm never coming back to Green?'" I asked. "New York's your favorite."

"I'll get another shot at it." Katy shrugged as she spoke and plopped down on a wicker ottoman. "I never thought I'd say this, but I miss Green. Being gone all the time isn't as much fun as it used to be."

Molly stood up slowly and steadied the swinging bed. "Katy knows what she's doing, Lois," she said, as though she were the grown-up. "It'll be OK."

"I'm in the room," Katy said. "I can explain. Not that I should have to explain."

"Of course you don't," I said. "I just want the best for you two. And Green doesn't have a lot going on right now."

"But you'll make something happen," Katy said. "You always do. Now may I go outside and hold little Eddie?" Before I could respond, she loped off.

"She didn't want to be gone this summer," Molly said. "After all that mess with the schools, she wanted to be home with her parents."

"I hate to be selfish," I said, "but it certainly will be good to have her here. The *Item* needs her."

As we strolled into the yard, we let the dogs—Holly Beth, joined by Markey, Kramer, and three-legged Mannix—out, and their joy was contagious. They sniffed, licked our legs, chased a ball that Molly threw, and romped with each other.

I studied the young women. Both seemed relaxed and happy. *"Lord, guide them,"* I prayed.

After thirty minutes or so, Mannix and Holly wore each other out, but the two bigger dogs continued their explorations. As usual, Mannix settled near Eddie, standing every few minutes to look at him before curling up again with Holly.

"So you're home for the entire summer, Katy?" Chris asked when I brought up the subject of her internship.

"Something like that."

"She won't admit it, but she's homesick," Molly chimed in.

"I admit it," Katy said and seemed to be gearing up for an argument, but paused instead to comfort Eddie, who waved his arms. He wore the miniature baseball uniform Tammy had given him. "I've had two years of college and three internships in New York, and I want to stay home this summer."

As she spoke, a red Jeep sped down Route Two. The sport vehicle zoomed past, stopped, jerked into reverse, and whipped into our driveway, kicking up more dust than Katy had.

"Who is that?" I asked, instinctively reaching for Eddie.

"Kids," Chris muttered and stood up to corral the dogs, who were putting on their impressive, but totally fake, guard-dog acts.

A tall, muscular young man climbed out of the truck with a quick wave, his long auburn hair pulled back in a ponytail, jeans torn at both knees, his UCLA T-shirt faded.

"Excuse me," he said in a deep voice.

"Whoa," Katy murmured, turning to look at Molly for a split second. "Where did he come from?"

"I seem to be turned around," the stranger said. His broad smile revealed the kind of straight white teeth that I had gotten from years of orthodontia, and his quick laugh seemed charming and self-deprecating. "I hate to admit it, but I need directions."

"You've come to the right place," I heard Katy whisper. "He's even better-looking than that old boss of Lois's."

The young man fished in his pocket and pulled out a crumpled piece of paper. Squinting, he adjusted his glasses slightly. That move should have made him look like a nerd, but it was clear that Molly and Katy would not use that word to describe him.

He spoke again. "I'm looking for Rev. Jean Hours at Grace Community Chapel. My GPS took me to that intersection down the road, but there's a highway where I thought the church was."

"Grace Chapel used to be there," Katy said, jumping up. "It got damaged in a tornado and moved around the corner. I can show you where it is, if you like." She tossed her hair, now the reddish color it had been when I first met her.

Chris stepped forward, and I recognized his coach-father routine kicking in. No way was he letting Katy go off with a strange guy without more information. "Chris Craig," he said, holding out his hand. "The church is only a couple of miles from here. I need to check in with Pastor Jean anyway, so you can follow me."

"Luke Tate," the young man said, shaking hands. "I'd appreciate the escort."

Unable to keep my curiosity at bay, I stood up, holding Eddie in one arm and extending my hand. "I'm Lois, Chris's wife. This is Molly and Katy."

"Nice to meet you," he said in a decidedly non-Louisiana accent. "Who's the little fellow?"

"That's Eddie," Katy said, as though she'd given birth to him herself. "Isn't he the cutest thing you've ever seen?"

Luke hesitated. "He's awfully small. I never quite know what to say about babies until they're big enough to throw a baseball or football."

"I know what you mean," Chris said. "All Eddie here wants to do is eat and sleep."

"He's very athletic," I protested, compelled to defend Eddie's five-month-old honor. "Look how he can kick."

Luke, who resembled Jesus in the Sunday school posters at my childhood church, chuckled and made eye contact with Chris. "Soccer player, you think? Or field-goal kicker?"

My husband laughed in a way that meant he had already taken to this Luke guy. "I coach at the high school, so I hope he's good at something," Chris said.

"So young and already so much pressure," I murmured.

Kissing Eddie's face and rubbing his soft hair, I looked back at the young man. "Why are you going to see Pastor Jean?" I asked, earning a "that-was-nosy" look from Chris and a whispered "finally" from Katy.

"I'm interested in the job," Luke said.

"The job?" I was puzzled.

"What job?" Katy asked.

"The pastor's job," he said.

Jean wiped her hands on a bright red dishtowel as she opened the door of the new parsonage.

"Why does that boy Luke think we have a pastor's job open?"

"Come on in, Lois, and tell me what's on your mind."

"Are you busy?" I asked, not the slightest bit embarrassed at barging in.

The only pastor I'd ever loved shook her head and smiled. "I've been expecting you ever since Luke told me he met you."

"What's going on with young Luke?" I said.

"Lois, he's not Eddie's age," she said. "You might not want to call him young Luke."

"He can't be a day over twenty-five," I said.

"I think it's pretty clear that Luke isn't a boy." She steered me to the living room, which meant this was more official than the usual chat around the kitchen table.

"Katy and Molly agree with you on that," I said.

"He may, in fact, be too good-looking to be a pastor," she said with a chuckle. For some reason, I had expected her mood to be more somber.

"Jean, you know I didn't come here to talk about how Luke Tate looks." I paced around the tidy room with its outdated floral sofa and overstuffed prayer chair. "Katy and Molly can take care of that part of this issue."

"So we've got an issue?"

"Only if you're leaving Grace." My face felt hot.

"Lois," Jean said in her gentle voice, the same voice that had counseled, encouraged, and chided me regularly during the last four years. That's all she said. My name. In that tone of voice.

The clock that made bird noises on each hour chirped like a cardinal. "We're about to have another of those spiritual discussions, aren't we?" I asked, sitting down. I slipped off my sandals and put my feet on the coffee table.

"I've thought about this and prayed about it, and I know it's getting close to time for me to go," Jean said.

"What does that mean?" I asked.

"It means I'm following God's direction," she answered.

"I don't want you to leave."

"I was pretty certain this wouldn't be your favorite idea," she said. "It won't happen for a while. I want to leave things in good order. Luke may have potential. We'll have to see."

"You're sure I can't talk you out of this?"

"I've prayed about this for more than a year," she said, "and moving back to Baton Rouge seems to be my answer. I never intended to live away from Don this long."

"I still don't understand why he doesn't quit the bank and move here."

"Lois, you're as stubborn as he is," Jean said. "He's got a good job with health insurance, and he wants to hang on until retirement."

"But God called you here," I said. "You guided Grace through the tornado and helped us relocate."

"I didn't," she said. "God did."

Exasperated, I clapped my hands together. "But God used you." I motioned to the room. "You even negotiated for the new parsonage. It's designed for you."

"Lois, you know more than most that things change. Every day. Things change."

She spoke so resolutely that I paused. I enjoyed our tough discussions, although sometimes I acted as though I didn't. In addition, I always felt like I was close to God in the silences between Jean and me.

The bird clock chirped again.

"Have you ever thought that God's call might change?" Jean asked after a few more minutes. Coming from someone else that question might have been rhetorical, but not from my pastor.

"Aren't calls forever?" I responded.

"Only two calls are forever: Love God with all your heart. Love your neighbor as yourself."

"That leaves a lot of leeway, doesn't it?" I said.

"It certainly does," Jean said, and her voice was almost a whisper. "Do you think the Lord could have different plans in mind for me at this stage in life?"

I knew what I wanted to say, but I also knew what I needed to say. "Jean, there's no telling how God might use you. You're an awesome preacher, and you know how to lead through crisis."

My mind could almost see the door closing on Jean's time in Green, but I plunged ahead. "I suppose we're called to different things at different points in our lives. A few years ago I'd never imagined having a baby, and now my life revolves around Eddie."

"Exactly," Jean said, as though I were a child who had just gotten the right answer in Sunday school. "God will direct me . . . and you and the rest of Grace Community."

"You've taught me that God always shows us the way," I said. "I believe that."

Jean chuckled. "It'd be nice for God to give us instructions on another stone tablet or a burning bush, wouldn't it? Sometimes we only get a nudge or a gut feeling . . . and that's enough."

"I'm afraid of getting my intuition tangled up," I said. "Aren't you?"

"That's one of the ways God teaches us," she said. "We have to sit down and listen, and step out on faith."

"God's too subtle for me at times," I said, and Jean laughed quietly.

"I didn't intend to mention all this quite yet," she said, "but a friend told me about Luke. I broached the possibility of an internship, with the idea it might grow into a full-time job. Next thing I know he's driving to North Louisiana from Seattle."

"So he drove all that way at the mention of a job?" I said. "That's crazy."

"Or faithful," Jean said. "I asked God to direct me, and the next day a friend mentioned Luke to me."

"That's only a coincidence," I protested. "Seminary graduates are always looking for jobs."

"Not at small rural churches in Northwest Louisiana. Young pastors have never contacted me, not even when that group from your friend's church came here on a mission trip."

"That still doesn't make it a divine sign."

"Maybe not," Jean agreed. "But it could be. Once I talked with Luke, I realized he's a good guy. And his references speak highly of him."

"So you seriously think this young preacher is a candidate to replace you?"

"That won't be my decision," she said. "I'm not leaving for a while, so we'll see how Luke works out. The church may decide to search for someone else. He could make a fine intern, either way. I made it clear to him that the job's not a certainty."

The small smile on her face grew. "Lois, there's growth in our church."

"That's because of you," I said. "You can't teach us those things and walk out." I closed my eyes for a moment. "It makes me sad to think of you leaving."

"I've learned more from you than you have from me," she said. "You're more than capable of handling life without me. You always were, but it's been good having each other. I count you as a dear friend."

I sniffed. "When people start thinking about moving, they move. That's how I wound up in Green. You won't be here much longer, will you?"

"I'll know when it's time, and I'll stand up and tell the church."

"I think I'll stay home that day."

"No, you won't," she said. "You'll sit up front where you always sit, and you'll smile, and you'll know that even though I'm leaving, God's staying."

"I'll pray for you," I said, the words not surprising me the way they used to. This new practice of prayer permeated my life, and I liked it. "And I'll pray for young Luke."

She grinned.

Our temporary intern was approved a week later, on Jean's recommendation.

"That's one of the benefits of a little church," Jean said, stopping by our house after church on Sunday. "Since Marti and Gary came with that crew of young people, our members have opened up a lot. The church can't pay him much, but he'll be fine as long as he has a place to stay."

Within two days, he'd settled in as a guest at my in-laws' house.

"We've got plenty of room," Hugh said when Chris, Eddie, and I stopped by after work one evening, "and I enjoy talking about the church's ministries with him."

Estelle chimed in. "Luke is an absolute joy to cook for." She almost giggled. "Says my biscuits are the best in the world."

"You already knew that," Chris said and patted his stomach. "Where do you think I got these extra pounds?"

"Oh, please," I said, looking at my husband's fit body.

"That young preacher's a big help to your father," Estelle said, and both my husband and father-in-law frowned at the same moment.

"What sort of help?" Chris asked.

"I don't need help," Hugh said.

"You're not getting any younger, Hugh," she said. "Luke mowed yesterday, and I saw him helping you with the cows."

"I told you I'd do that after baseball practice," Chris said.

Hugh waved his hand, as though dismissing a room full of people. "Son, you've got a wife and a baby and a job and a house to finish. Luke's earning his keep."

As if we had summoned him, the preacher tapped on the kitchen door and came in, taking his tennis shoes off at the door. "Mud," he said.

"He'd better hope it's mud," I whispered.

"Come on in," Estelle said, beaming. "Hugh and I were telling our son and daughter-in-law how much we enjoy having you around."

"Are you sure I'm not intruding?" he asked.

"Not at all," Hugh said. "Come see my fine grandson."

Chris stood and greeted Luke with enthusiasm. "Thanks for helping Dad out," he said. "I meant to get over here earlier and take care of this yard."

"I needed the exercise," Luke said. "I sat in on Pastor Jean's Bible study this morning and helped with church paperwork this afternoon, so I was cooped up all day."

While he talked, I looked him over. Somehow, in less than a week he had become part of our lives. I wanted to be skeptical, but I knew to my core that this was a man of God.

"Knock, knock," Katy called, punctuating my thoughts. "Anybody home?"

She glowed as she hugged Estelle at the front door and held out a baby-blue gift bag. "More loot," she said, swinging the bag back and forth from her fingers. "My mother asked me to deliver it to Eddie."

"And you couldn't wait until work tomorrow?" I said under my breath. Chris looked at Katy looking at Luke and met my gaze, a twinkle in his eyes.

"I went by your house, but you weren't home," she said, as though that explained why she'd shown up here.

Estelle went into full party mode, pulling out a fresh strawberry cake. "I made this for my ladies group," she said, "but I'll whip another one up tomorrow. I love having company."

"I'll help serve," Katy said, swirling around the room with saucers and forks, making an extra trip for napkins and always spending a minute longer in front of Luke than any of the rest of us.

"Hugh, this is like when our kids were young," Estelle said.

"Did girls come over to flirt with you?" I whispered to Chris, pretending to check the baby.

"More times than I can count," he said with a smile.

"Should we be worried about Katy and Luke?" I asked.

Chris looked back at Katy, who had settled onto the couch next to Luke.

"Without a doubt," he said.

5

Martha Reeves was surprised by one of the letters written during a penmanship lesson in her third-grade class at Green Elementary School. "Jaden McDade's letter said, 'Dear President: Thank you for not closing my school. I was afraid I might get lost at a new school because of all the halls. Schools are big. Love, Jaden. P.S. Mrs. Reeves is a real good teacher.'"

—The Green News-Item

In a town filled with people I cared about, Jerry Turner was an ongoing challenge. After losing the mayor's race to Eva Hillburn by only a handful of votes, Jerry had turned into a grouch.

Maybe he'd always been a grouch, come to think about it.

As a banker, he liked to throw his employer's weight around. As a political wannabe, he liked to criticize Eva, the newspaper, and anyone or anything else that didn't "do to suit him," as Tammy said.

When he showed up at the newspaper in the middle of June, I wished I'd had more warning. Zach had called four times for appointments, and I was putting him off. I would have put Jerry on that same list.

Without waiting for Tammy to announce him, Eva's enemy strode into my office wearing the seersucker suit only a small tier of Green executives donned each summer. Carrying a briefcase, he would have looked quaint to some, but to me he seemed pretentious.

"Miss Lois," he boomed in an overly cheerful voice, "I need a few minutes of your time."

"I'm in the middle of something at the moment." I tried to add a note of regret to my voice and made a show of shuffling a stack of papers on my desk, thankful that Eddie and Ellie, both in my office today, were asleep. "Can this wait?"

Jerry frowned, a powerful enough businessman that he was rarely told "no." "You're going to want to hear about this," he said. "It affects the good citizens of Green."

While I tried to decide whether to let him sit down or reschedule, Holly Beth dashed in from the newsroom and jumped up on him. Jerry pushed her down roughly and brushed his pants off. Holly Beth growled and stalked around my office, as though considering peeing.

"Holly Beth!" I hissed and turned to Jerry. "Sorry. Holly was so spoiled before Eddie came along that she looks for a reason to throw a fit."

"I leave my dog at home," Jerry said. "That keeps this sort of thing from happening."

Not responding, I motioned to one of the armchairs in front of my desk and settled into the chair behind my desk, deciding I might as well get this over with.

As I sat, I noticed I had Eddie's spit-up cloth draped over my left shoulder. Yanking it off, I couldn't resist fingering the monogram that Pearl Taylor, Kevin's mother, had sewn. I could smell a hint of baby powder.

Jerry snapped open his briefcase, each clasp making a popping noise. Lifting the top, he pulled out a neatly labeled folder, then closed the case and set it aside. "Eva Hillburn activities," the printed label read. He removed a sheaf of papers from it, including newspaper clippings taped neatly on copy paper, and a brochure for a municipal government conference.

"I realize you are personal friends with the mayor," he said, making the words sound like an accusation. "But it is the responsibility of the local newspaper to investigate public improprieties."

His voice rose as he spoke, and I alternated between anger at his implications and worry that he would wake the children. "There's no need to shout, Jerry," I said. I motioned toward the cribs behind him. "Eddie and Ellie are with me and Iris today. They're sleeping."

Turning his head, a look of surprise and then annoyance passed over his face. "So you bring your children to work, too?" he said. "Well, isn't that unusual."

"On-site child care," I said. "Having them here is a nice perk of running the *Item*."

"I want the newspaper to look into how the mayor's office is spending taxpayer money," he said, obviously tired of talking about newspaper day care. "I have documentation that Eva Hillburn is taking personal vacations with public dollars."

"Eva wouldn't do that." My voice rose, "She's the most ethical elected official I've ever known."

"I wouldn't be so sure about that," Jerry said. "Her boyfriend had a run-in with the law, and her brother is a convicted felon."

"Neither of those cases involved Eva. I'm very aware of Dub and Major's problems, but they involved me, not the mayor."

Jerry reached into his pocket and pulled out a pair of reading glasses, slipping them onto his nose and peering at the brochure he held. "Have you talked to your friend the mayor about the business she did in Florida back in the spring?" he asked, putting air quotes around the word *business* and grimacing when he said the word *mayor*.

"Eva's been out of town a lot," I said, but regretted the words. "And my work schedule has shifted since I had a child."

"So you've not been in touch with Mayor Hillburn?"

I sat up straighter and adjusted my skirt. "You sound like an attorney," I said. "What's your point?"

"My point is that the mayor of Green owes it to the town to show up for work, and should not be gallivanting all over the country with citizens picking up the check." He paused as if for dramatic effect. "She's also not returning calls on her cell phone, which, I might point out, is paid for out of the city budget. I would hope the local newspaper would investigate this travesty and let readers know what is going on."

I rubbed a small spot of spit-up on my sleeve, as I formulated what to say. "Jerry, half the citizens of Green have a conspiracy theory, an expose, or a Pulitzer-Prize winning scoop for the *Item* to report on. If we chased every rumor that sails into this building, we'd never get the paper out."

"But you chase some of them, don't you?"

"Of course we do," I said. "That's how Major Wilson and Dub McCuller wound up in trouble with the law, as you are well aware."

"Then why not look into what the mayor's up to?"

"Because there's nothing to look into," I said. "We cover city government thoroughly, despite our small staff. Eva is an outstanding leader."

"Lots of folks are talking about this, Lois, and it would be a public service to clear it up," he said and then waved his right hand, as though the subject was of no consequence. "Not that it matters to me one way or the other."

"If it doesn't matter to you, then why are you sitting here talking about it?"

"I'm going to be the next mayor," he said. "People aren't going to stand for this kind of government. I am bringing that industrial park downtown, along with much-needed jobs."

My head ached. "Jerry, that hideous industrial park is *not* the answer to Green's troubles. It will ruin the charm of downtown."

"Charm?" he said, in a tone that very much reminded me of the late Chuck McCuller, who had owned the *Item*. "We have a scummy lake, empty stores, and a decline in sales tax collections. Where is the charm in any of that?"

I sat up straighter, put my elbows on the desk, and looked into his eyes. "The lake problem is temporary." *I hoped.* "Downtown merchants are exploring options to draw traffic here." *Sort of.* "And Mayor Hillburn is a fiscally responsible leader. She will guide us through needed changes." *For sure.*

"Hmmph," Jerry said. "If you weren't so stubborn, you'd look into this, and you'd find out the truth about our so-called mayor and the importance of this industrial park."

I stood up. "I don't try to run your bank, and I'd appreciate your not trying to run this newspaper."

"Your Post Media colleague doesn't feel the same way," Jerry said. "If you won't cover it, he'll be more than happy to. Zach recognizes the value of the industrial park." He placed the file folder on my desk. "Here is a copy of the documentation I've given him. Maybe it'll be useful when you decide to report the news instead of doing PR for your friends."

My heart was pounding when he left, reminiscent of early encounters with both Chuck and Dub McCuller, who had tried to run me out of town from this very office. Walking over to the cribs, I looked in on the babies. Eddie's big brown eyes, exactly like Chris's, opened.

"What do you think, Edward? What should I do?"

"I hate to break this to you," Tammy said from behind me, "but Eddie can't talk."

"And here I was hoping he'd tell me what to do about a big story." I reached in to pick him up. "I'll have to ask you instead."

"I'm a photographer, not a reporter," Tammy said, fidgeting with one of her many strands of chunky, colored beads. She looked wary. "Where's Linda? Shouldn't you talk to her about this?"

I sank into one of the chairs, loving the soft, warm feel of Eddie in my arms. "Linda's covering the Police Jury meeting this afternoon and helping Iris with advertising contracts." I sighed. "What I wouldn't give for another staff member or two."

"You and me both," Tammy said. "So, what's on your mind? Jerry Turner didn't come in here for a social visit."

Through my years as a journalist, I'd learned to be cautious with allegations. They hung over people, and rumors spread faster than the paint I'd spilled on my kitchen floor while remodeling. I hated to start this ball rolling.

"Is this about Mayor Eva?" Tammy asked before I spoke.

"You've heard?"

"Pretty ugly gossip is going around about her spending city money on private travel. Plus, the business types are talking about going over her head to get that industrial park on the edge of downtown."

Tammy acted as though she were about to reach for Eddie, but then leaned over to pet Holly Beth, who had strolled out of her crate and was stretching like a yoga expert.

"Jerry wants the *Item* to investigate," I said. "He says he's got Zach on his side."

"Could there be any truth to his concerns? You're the one who always says where there's smoke, there's fire."

"We're talking about Eva Hillburn here, not Richard Nixon," I said. "No one cares about Green as much as she does."

Tammy patted her lap, and Holly jumped up, looking at Eddie and then me as though making it clear she had chosen the photographer's lap over mine.

"Walt heard the rumors at the courthouse in Shreveport," Tammy said. "A developer asked him why Green was demolishing historic buildings to put in an industrial park."

"We have to clear this up," I said. "This newspaper's got to stop these lies."

"You'll find out what's going on," she said. "You always do."

I looked down at Eddie in my arms, so innocent, so pure. "It's hard," I said.

"I know," she replied, her manner kinder than I expected.

Ellie started whimpering.

"Will you get her?" I asked. "Iris Jo's gone to the post office."

Tammy's soft streak disappeared, and she almost bolted from my office. "I'll see if I can find Stan. I'll be right back."

"Stan'll be covered in ink," I said, but she was already headed for the pressroom.

"It is simply not possible," I said to Chris as we strolled down Route Two after dinner that night. "Is it?"

"We've seen pretty weird things happen since you showed up in Green," Chris said with a small smile.

"You make it sound like I'm a plague or something."

"I wouldn't put it like that," he said, "but we've had fires, thefts, and a tornado since you arrived." He dropped a kiss on my hair. "Nonetheless, you're the best thing that ever happened to me."

"You're the one person I know who can warm my heart with an insult."

Pushing Eddie's stroller, my husband maneuvered around a big rock on the road. He softly chided Kramer, the biggest of the dogs, who was attacking a piece of plastic in the ditch. Mannix, Chris's three-legged dog who had saved a life after the tornado, hung back near Eddie and Holly Beth. I knew without a doubt Mannix was guarding his family.

While I talked, I checked for the tenth time to make sure Eddie wasn't being "eaten alive" by mosquitoes, as his Grandma Estelle often warned me to do. When I covered him with a thin blanket, I worried he'd suffocate. When I removed it, I feared West Nile virus.

The June night was hot but not stifling, and the air smelled of tilled soil and honeysuckle. The sun had nearly disappeared, leaving an orange glow through the tree lines past one of Chris's catfish ponds. Frogs were in full voice, and an owl hooted in the distance.

"It's so beautiful out here," I said. "So peaceful. I don't want to imagine something bad going on."

"Eva's honest," Chris said. "These are exaggerations by someone who wants to stir things up. You know how Green is. If there's nothing interesting to talk about, people make something up."

"How am I going to stay on top of this?" I asked. "My to-do list is already longer than the new bypass."

After I did another mosquito check on Eddie, we headed back toward the house.

A weird feeling came over me two days later when I stepped into Eva's office at her department store. She was on the phone, and the office had been rearranged with a new impressionistic painting of a couple walking on a beach. Her dark wooden antique desk anchored the room, and she sat behind it, toying with a letter opener with a deep blue handle.

"Lois," the mayor said as she hung up, walking around the desk and peering over my shoulder. "I was delighted when I heard you'd set up a visit. Where's that baby boy of yours?"

I fidgeted with a button on the summer suit I'd pulled out for the meeting. "Eddie's at the paper with Iris and Ellie. I wasn't sure whether to bring him or not."

"Nonsense," Eva said in her usual matter-of-fact style. "Business is done in entirely different ways these days. He's always welcome."

"I suppose," I said, "but it's hard for me to focus when he's around."

"He must have grown a foot while I was gone," she said. "Dub and I are both eager to see him."

"Did you have a good trip?" I asked. "Or should I say trips?"

She motioned me to an upholstered wingback chair and returned to her leather desk chair. "Parts of the trips were lovely," she said, "but the conference was tedious. Everyone has an idea on how to save small towns, the more outlandish the better. Frankly, I felt like it was a waste of my time."

Holding up a stack of pink telephone messages and a file folder, she shook her head. "Between making sure garbage gets picked up and taking complaints about speeding on the bypass, I've been inundated."

"For a small place, there's always a lot going on," I said, not meeting her gaze.

"Do you have something on your mind?" Eva asked, a slight frown wrinkling her forehead.

"On my mind?"

She tapped her head with a manicured finger, as though reminding me where my brain was. "You called for an appointment. I hoped you had new thoughts on dealing with the lake and the highway."

"The lake and the highway?" I parroted.

"We've got to come up with something to stop the decline downtown, but I adamantly oppose Jerry's industrial park. It will destroy the character of our town."

I drew in a breath. "Thank goodness."

She looked perplexed. "You and I have a similar vision for downtown Green, unless you've changed your mind. What's going on here?"

"The *Item's* getting complaints about your recent travel," I said so quickly my words ran together. I reorganized my thoughts and plunged ahead. "Rumors are swirling around town, accusing you of vacationing on your city expense account and neglecting your duties."

Half-expecting the ceiling to fall in, I edged to the front of the chair and tried to emulate her posture. "Eva, I trust you completely, but the *Item* needs a statement."

She stood up, her palms on her desk. The last time I had seen this pose was right before she threw her ex-husband out of the office when he'd tried to shut down Green's school. "Jerry Turner is accusing me of malfeasance," she said. "He wants my job."

"Eva, Jerry's leading the complaints, but everyone's on edge . . ."

". . . And they're looking for someone to blame," she said, finishing my sentence.

"Jerry's telling everyone how expensive the hotel in Florida was and how you took Dub with you to a meeting that was a big political junket."

"There's more, isn't there?" she asked, sitting back down.

I pulled out a photograph of Eva and Dub arm-in-arm in evening clothes on the beach, the sun a fiery ball beside them. Major Wilson, fresh out of jail, strolled beside them, an unidentified woman next to him. Someone had typed an orange headline on the top, reading "Your Tax $$$ at work!?!"

"This started flying around the Internet yesterday." I tried to force a chuckle, which came out sounding like a rusty gate swinging open. "To hear Jerry tell it, you've been dancing and drinking champagne and basically living the life of Jackie Onassis."

"This nonsense sure gets old," she said, taking the photo from my outstretched hands. "Some days I think I should sell my store, retire from public office, play golf with Dub, and not care what people say—or think."

"That'd be terrible!" I exclaimed.

Eva laughed. "You're the only person in the world who would say that. You're one of those people who love their jobs. I wish there were more like you."

"You love politics," I said. "That other life wouldn't make you happy. It's not you."

"Not most days, although it sounds pretty good today." She walked around the desk and gracefully lowered herself into the chair next to mine. "I may not be mayor much longer," she said.

"What?" My head spun so quickly toward her that my neck hurt.

"But it won't be because of petty Jerry." She tapped her nails on the edge of the elegant desk. "I'm running for Congress. I'm determined to make a difference in this tired old world of ours."

6

A vanload of students traveled to Little Rock for a competition billed as the "craziest day of your life." However, it wasn't the leaping over flames or crawling through dark trenches that was most difficult. A storm hit during the last obstacle, and the students took cover in a ditch. "We were unable to let them approach the course again," the director said, "even though they explained about the experience they had gone through in Green."

—The Green News-Item

My threats to contact a national preservation group stopped the demolition of the historic ice-cream stand. Except I hadn't exactly had the idea. Yet.

Tammy cornered Major Wilson on Main Street and proclaimed my intentions. She insisted it was all my idea, and I would not be stopped.

I learned of my intentions when Tammy walked into the newsroom with Becca on her heels.

"These tulips are for you, Lois," Tammy said. "We know how much you like them." She set the vase on the vacant desk where Eddie slept in his carrier, and I moved them to a scarred end table next to the coffeepot.

After admiring the deep pink blooms, I eyed the women suspiciously. "You have never once given me flowers, Tammy. What's the occasion?"

"They're, sort of," she hemmed and hawed, reminding me of my recent visit to Eva's office, "sort of a peace offering."

"Did we have a fight?" I asked.

"Not yet," she said, "but we might in a minute."

"Tammy told Major you're investigating his lakefront development project and might file suit," Becca said. "She sort of mentioned you're planning a community rally to save the Bayou Freez and are contacting an organization up North."

"And it worked!" Tammy tried high-fiving the florist, who looked taken aback.

"Shhh," I said, nodding over at Eddie and wondering what Tammy had stirred up. "I want to finish today's editorial before he wakes up."

"I doubt a freight train would wake him up," Tammy said.

"Major wouldn't listen until Tammy brought up your name and the preservationists," Becca said. "Then he started shouting that he'd rather face another prison term than be caught in a room with you and a bunch of history nuts."

"Nice to see that jail mellowed him," I said, thankful that I'd not run into him since his release. "I don't know how I'm going to take on this crusade when I can't even get my laundry done."

"But you're so good at challenges," Tammy said. "You're the only one who can keep Major from tearing the Freez down."

"If he does that'll just be the start," Becca said. "Once he tears down one old building, research shows that others will be abandoned or razed. An industrial park first and then an abandoned downtown. Abandoned."

Tammy plopped down at one of our handful of computers. "Let me show you the photos I took today. They're going to help save one of the oldest buildings in Green. I never noticed all these details until Becca pointed them out."

"It's one of a kind," Becca said.

"We have two weeks to change Major's mind," Tammy said, scrolling through the photo gallery she'd downloaded.

"Since you figured out how to stall him, I'm sure you'll be able to figure out how to stop him," I said, looking over Tammy's shoulders at the compelling photographs.

"This has escalated so fast," Becca said. "Green needs you to do this, Lois."

I leaned over and studied the photos. "That is a special building, isn't it?"

I saw Tammy share a knowing look with Becca.

"Chris is going to kill me," I said.

"Phooey," Tammy said, pulling her hair back and securing it with a rubber band from a desk drawer. "This has Lois Barker Craig written all over it. Think what a boost this will be for downtown."

"I wonder if we need to contact Walt about an injunction?" I asked, admiring a shot of the stucco building, an orange trumpet vine blooming at the base of the old-fashioned ice cream cone sign.

"Yes!" Tammy said with a fist pump to Becca. "I told you Lois could handle it."

"I don't know," Becca said, her look worried. "I wouldn't be surprised if Major tore it down with his bare hands. That man will do anything." She pursed her lips. "I've just never understood why he's like that."

"Because he can be," Tammy said. "He nearly got Lois killed by not ratting on his friend Chuck, and he wouldn't let African Americans move into his fancy neighborhoods."

"That's ancient history," I said. "He says he's changed since jail."

Tammy rolled her eyes at me as the bell on the door into the lobby chimed. She started back to her post just as Major himself stuck his head into the newsroom. "Anyone home?" he asked in his jovial politician's voice.

Holly Beth, who had been asleep on a cushion Molly and Katy had bought her, jumped up and flew at Major, barking. Eddie whimpered. Major looked down at the dog with a grimace and said, "Sugar Marie?"

"Her puppy." I tried to quiet the dog, watching Eddie stirring out of the corner of my eye. "Your sister gave her to me for a wedding gift."

"One of the many things I missed while I was in jail." Major shook his head. "Eva thinks that dog of hers hung the moon. Personally I don't see the point in dogs that are too little to take hunting."

"We were telling Lois you agreed not to tear down the dairy stand," Tammy said.

"I wouldn't go that far," Major said. "I said I'd hold off for two weeks and see if you can come up with a buyer."

"A buyer?" I asked.

"If people are so all-fired in love with this building, then let them pay for it. I lost a lot of money after the paper sent me to jail. I can't sit on that prime real estate because some do-good group pretends to love it."

When Major launched into one of his tirades, I was always torn between laughing in his face and running in terror. His beefy face reddened, and beads of sweat broke out on his forehead. "If you ask me, downtown Green needs all the help it can get," he said. "Getting rid of this falling down piece of junk will be a good start. Then we can build nice new buildings."

"It's not falling down," Becca said. "The building only needs a little TLC."

"Exactly why are *you* in my face about this?" Major asked the younger woman. "I thought you and that no-good brother of yours lived in Ashland."

Tammy and I exchanged a look.

"You two know each other?" I asked.

"Not very well," Becca said.

"All too well," Major said at the same time.

"My brother used to do odd jobs for him," Becca said.

"Have you seen our friend Lee Roy Hicks?" Major asked. "I heard he's out of the hoosegow too."

Becca threw me a beseeching look. "I lost touch with him a few years ago."

This conversation got more interesting by the second. Major Wilson and Lee had been big buddies in the past and both had done time for their wrongs. Lee seemed to have reformed, but Major could never make me believe he was on the up and up.

Eddie started crying, his voice sounding like a cross between a cat and the printer when it jammed.

"Well, well, well, what have we got here?" Major's voice changed as he noticed the baby for the first time. "Is this Chris Craig's boy?"

Tammy stepped closer to the baby, as though shielding him. "I believe we were talking about you destroying a downtown landmark."

"I'm not aiming to make trouble, ladies, but I also don't intend to lose my shirt on this deal," Major said. "There's big changes coming to downtown Green, and I want to be in on them. You have two weeks to make me change my mind. That's fourteen full days. Otherwise, that building is going to be a different kind of history."

He headed for the door, and Becca scurried after him. "I need to get back to my shop," she said. "I'll see Major out."

I lifted Eddie from the carrier, while Tammy moved one of the window blinds to look out into the parking lot.

"They're talking," she whispered, as though they might hear her. "Becca's trying to walk off, but he's holding onto her arm. That's weird because she didn't say anything to him when we were at the Bayou Freez earlier."

"Is he hurting her?" I rushed over to the window with the baby. "Let me see."

"Major's leaving, and Becca looks upset," Tammy said.

As we watched, the man climbed into a shiny new pickup and drove off. "That's weird," Tammy repeated as Linda, reporter and bookkeeper, walked in from the business office.

"What are you two looking at?" she asked, picking up a neat stack of notes from her desk.

"Major Wilson just paid us his first post-jail visit," I said.

"No wonder you look tense," Linda said.

"Becca was here, too," Tammy added. "It was like they had some sort of history. He even mentioned Lee Hicks."

Linda turned away from her computer. "They used to date," she said.

"Becca and Major?" My words didn't come close to registering the dismay I felt.

"Becca and Lee," Linda said. "People say she's the one who broke up his marriage."

"She doesn't strike me as the home-wrecker type," I protested.

"I never could figure it out, but she stopped by the office every now and then when I worked for Major," Linda said. "She was crazy in love with Lee."

"The other day when we saw Lee, she acted like she hardly knew him," I said.

"Maybe she had a change of heart when he went to jail." Tammy snorted. "She probably doesn't want to hurt her reputation as a business owner."

As Tammy was leaving work for the day, I called her into my office.

"Thank you," I said, "for looking out for Eddie when Major was in the newsroom. He made me nervous."

She shrugged, her skirt and blouse wrinkled after a day of work. "I don't think Major'd ever hurt the little guy, but I didn't like him getting close."

"You never get very close to Eddie either," I said, broaching the subject that weighed on me.

"That's not true," she said. "I'm around him all day, every day."

"But you don't get close to him." The fear of someone not liking my child was a new one, and I wasn't quite sure how to handle it.

Tammy took a deep breath. "Do we have to have this conversation now? I wanted to get home before Walt and put supper on to cook."

"Have it your way." I couldn't stop myself as she headed for the door, "But I always thought you'd be like an aunt to my child, be crazy about him and Ellie."

She stopped and turned around, an upset look aimed at me. "I'm too crazy about him," she said. "I've been trying to get pregnant ever since Eddie was born, and it's not working." She walked over to the portable crib. "Every time I look at him, I worry I'll never be able to give Walt a child of his own."

When I pulled in after work, Major Wilson stood in our front yard talking to Lee. Holly Beth ran over to greet Lee as soon as I let her out of the SUV, and she rolled around on her back, waiting for his greeting before growling at Major and running back to the fence where the other three dogs raced up and down.

"I didn't expect to see you here, Major," I said over my shoulder as I wrestled the baby out of the car, still raw after Tammy's words.

"I was in the area and thought I'd check on my hunting trailer," he said.

"Let me help you with that, Lois," Lee said, coming to the side of the vehicle and taking the heavy carrier, while I got the diaper bag, my purse, and the other items that daily made me feel like a pack mule.

Major watched intently, but didn't walk our way. "It slipped my mind that Lee Roy was living in the travel trailer," he said.

"Especially since the trailer was being used as a meth lab," Lee said sharply.

"We didn't learn until later that you're not supposed to live in a place again after that," I said. "Did you ever hear who had that lab out there in the woods, Major?" I had to admit I enjoyed jabbing the annoying man.

"Some kids in the woods is what I heard," Major said, cutting his eyes over to Lee. "No one I'd ever heard of. Lee Roy, maybe you know something about all that." His tone was sly.

I looked at Lee, the man who had once attacked me in the newspaper parking lot, now holding my baby as carefully as if it were his own. I wasn't sure what Major was implying, but I wasn't going to put up with it. "Lee's a good man," I said. "We enjoy having him nearby. Eddie and Holly Beth are crazy about him."

"This boy means the world to me," Lee said. "He's the next best thing to having a child of my own." Holly ran up, clearly jealous of Lee holding Eddie, and Lee laughed. "Chris and Lois have been awfully good to me, and I won't ever forget it."

"You've done a lot for us, too," I said, wondering why I would trust my former enemy with my baby's life but not want Major Wilson to come within a hundred yards of him.

"Lee Roy and I were comparing notes on our time away when you drove up," Major said. Regrettably, he followed us up to the porch. "No matter what anyone tells you, those white-collar jails aren't any country club."

The early evening air ruffled my long hair, and I reached over to check on Eddie.

"I don't think Major and I share the same opinion on our sentences," Lee said. "If it hadn't been for jail, I'm not sure I'd have ever turned my life around and gotten my faith back."

"Hmmph," Major said. "I don't believe in jailhouse religion."

"Believe what you will," Lee said quietly, "but I was one messed-up man, and Mr. Hugh and others led me back." Wearing his construction clothes, with the sunset bouncing off his face, he was handsome and appealing. "I wish I could undo all the wrong I did."

"At least *you're* trying," I said and threw a pointed look at Major.

Major flashed a big, toothy smile. "I haven't been back in Green but a few weeks, and Miss Lois is already mad at me."

"Major, you have been known to rub folks the wrong way," Lee said.

Major laughed as though that were the funniest thing he'd ever heard. "Takes one to know one."

The dogs yelped, their alert that Chris was approaching, and my husband's old truck pulled into sight. While I was always glad to see him, today I was downright thrilled.

He honked once and stepped out with the special smile he saved for me and Eddie before turning to Major. "I never know who's going to turn up around here," he said, extending his hand. "Welcome back."

"Good to be back, son." Major shook his hand as vigorously as if he were getting water from an old pump. "That's a fine boy you have there."

Chris walked over to where Eddie and I stood, giving each of us a brief kiss. "This boy's turned our world upside down," he said.

"You've done a fine job with your renovation project here," Major said. "This is the first time I've been out on Route Two in some time. It doesn't even look like the same place."

"Lois and I appreciate the loan of the trailer," Chris said. "For a while there, we thought we might be out on the street. There was so much going on, we weren't sure what we wanted to do. The trailer bought us some time."

"Now that Major's back, we need to get it back to him," Lee said, looking right at the other man. "It's probably time I find a place of my own."

"But, Lee," I said, "we agreed you'd stay until the house is finished."

"And what will Holly do without you?" Chris said with a grin as the dog frolicked nearby.

"No rush," Major said. "I won't be hunting anytime soon." He looked at Lee. "No guns for either of us, I suppose."

"Never was much of a hunter anyway," Lee said and walked toward the small tractor that sat nearby, talking as he went. "I'd better get back to the yard before it gets dark."

"I never thought I'd see the day when Lee Roy Hicks would do manual labor," Major said. "He acts like a different person."

"It's not an act," Chris said. "He's a better man."

"Thank goodness we all get second chances," I said, wondering how to get Major to leave.

"Why don't you come in and have supper with us?" my big-hearted husband asked.

Behind Major's back, I scowled at Chris, but he only smiled and started for the door. "Lee and the rest of that crew have done a great job on the house, and we like to show it off."

"I'd like to see it," Major said. "I love these old buildings." His eyes met mine, and he gave me a quick wink.

While they looked around, I pulled a casserole from the freezer, thankful for my mother-in-law, who worried about our meals, and got Eddie ready for bed. By the time supper was ready, Chris and Major had finished their tour, and Chris called for Lee to join us, the smell of mown grass coming through the open door. With Eddie tucked in for the night, the four of us sat around the kitchen table.

"I understand you went to Florida after you were released, Major," I said.

"I met Eva and Dub down there and stayed to golf with a cousin from Alabama," he said, chewing on a piece of my cornbread with his eyes closed. "This may be the best thing I've ever eaten."

For a split second I had a warm feeling toward our annoying guest. Chris patted my hand, and I knew he recognized my struggle to accept Major at our table. My husband was far kinder than I was.

"My sister told me she was none too happy about people digging around in her personal business about that trip," Major continued, and my warm feeling disappeared. "Just because I got in a little trouble doesn't mean Eva's done anything wrong."

I wiped my mouth and muttered into the napkin. Chris nudged my foot under the table.

"What most people don't know," Chris said, "is how hard it is for the newspaper to do its job. Lois agonizes over every negative story, and someone's always aggravated with her and her staff."

Lee smiled and nodded. "It's probably a lot like your job as a coach."

"She aggravated me today, that's for sure," Major said, using what I thought of as his pretend voice. "She's trying to save that dump of an ice-cream stand. Her and Tammy and that Becca woman you used to hang out with, Lee Roy, telling me it shouldn't be torn down."

Lee choked on his iced tea. "Sorry," he apologized. "That went down the wrong way."

"Are you talking about the Bayou Freez, Major?" Chris asked.

"One and the same," he said. "Me and Jerry have big plans for that property."

"That place was the hangout when I was a kid," Chris said. "I spent every dime I had on their milkshakes."

"I didn't know that," I said.

"As a matter of fact," Chris said, "I could use one of those milkshakes right now. They don't come like that anymore."

"I haven't thought about those in years," Major said. "Chuck, Dub, Eva, and I used to head over there every summer night when we were teenagers. That's been a long time ago."

Lee seemed to have recovered from the choking incident. "That place closed when I was a kid," he chimed in. "I'd almost forgotten it was there until we got the work order on it."

"Well, Miss Lois here noticed it," Major said. "She doesn't think I should tear it down."

"That's exactly right," I said and threw Chris what I hoped was an irresistible smile. "I think my husband and I should buy it."

7

Four golfers claim to have made holes-in-one on the first day of the month at the Oak Creek Country Club. "Our restaurant promised free burgers to anyone who made the rare shot, and they came out of the woodwork," Golf Pro Jason Butts said. "But your shot must be verified." The club's oldest golfer, Evelyn Mitchell, said she didn't care if her first hole-in-one was recorded or not. "I saw it go in that hole, and that's all that matters. I don't care for the burgers here anyway."

—The Green News-Item

Kevin coerced me into going out for dinner at the Country Club.

"Let's be wild," she said on the phone. "You can wear makeup and everything."

"I don't remember how to be wild," I said, laughing. "Come to think of it, I never was any good at being wild."

"At least think about it," she said. "Terrence has a business meeting, and you and I never have Girls Night Out. You don't even make it to the quilting group anymore."

"You know how it is," I said. "When you adopted Asa, your whole routine changed."

"The good news is it gets easier as they get older. Asa wants to fix his own breakfast since he turned four. He keeps reminding me he's a big boy."

"Eddie pretty much wants me to fix all his meals," I said. "And then he wants to stay up half the night and play."

"He'll grow out of that," she said. "How about it? Tonight. Country Club. Six o'clock."

"I don't see how I can," I said. "With the catfish ponds and practices, Chris gets in late. We need to work on the house. Maybe another time."

"Lois Barker Craig, how old is your son?"

I didn't have to stop and figure. "Almost seven months."

"And how many times have we gotten together since he was born?"

"You've been out to the house twice," I said, "but I've been to your office three or four times."

"Doctor's visits don't count," she said. "Thank goodness I'm Eddie's pediatrician, or I'd have to find a new best friend."

"It's hard to leave Eddie," I said. "I'm already figuring out how to go to college with him."

Kevin's comforting physician's voice matched her beautiful looks. "Most mothers of infants feel that way," she said. "Bring Eddie with you. That way we get to visit, and you'll be able to watch your son."

"When you say it like that, it sounds a little obsessive," I said. "Where's Asa staying?"

"You know he'll be with Mama and Daddy. I have to argue to take him home at night. They haven't forgiven me for not moving in with them after the tornado."

Kevin's parents, Pearl and Marcus Taylor, were the first people to invite me to their home for dinner when I moved to Green. The entire family held a large spot in my heart.

"Are they still trying to convince you to marry Terrence?" I asked.

"Of course! They adore him."

"And you?" I asked. "Has he convinced you yet?"

Kevin groaned. "If you want to start digging into my love life, you have to meet me for dinner."

"OK. OK." I capitulated. "Chris has a coach's meeting. Let me check with Estelle and Hugh and see if they'll watch Eddie. They complain that I don't bring him over enough, so they'll be thrilled."

"I suspect your husband will appreciate the break," Kevin said. "He can do something with the guys."

"He needs that, for sure," I said. "When you add Eddie and remodeling to coaching and catfish, he doesn't get much down time."

By late afternoon, everyone but me seemed delighted by the evening's developments. Chris planned to grab a burger with his volunteers, and my mother-in-law acted like Eddie lived six-hundred miles away and was making a rare appearance.

Even Tammy congratulated me on my plans.

"This scamp needs a break from his hovering mother," she said, picking Eddie up from his crib in my office. Since her confession about not being able to get pregnant, she had treated Eddie and Ellie like everyone else did, which basically meant spoiling them rotten.

"He's a newborn," I said. "You make it sound like I should give him the keys to the car."

"He's an infant, not a newborn, and there is a distinction," she said. "Do you want him to grow up to be a mama's boy?"

"Of course I do," I said without cracking a smile.

Tammy burst into laughter and nuzzled Eddie, who smiled up at her, his brown eyes shining. He was so cute that I wanted to take him right out of her arms and cuddle him myself.

Oak Crest Country Club was nearly empty when Kevin and I arrived, and the manager directed us to the dining room. "You pretty much have your pick of tables," he said. "We've got reservations for two others, but other than that, we're empty tonight."

"Where is everyone?" I asked.

"Beats me," he said. "If something doesn't change, we're going to have to close on weeknights. I can't afford to pay the staff for these kinds of numbers."

"I'm hearing that from the people who come to the clinic, too," Kevin said. "They're scared."

She sat regally in the chair the waiter pulled out, as though we were in a five-star restaurant in New York City. Her hair was pulled back in its usual elegant French twist, and she wore a pair of dress trousers with a chiffon blouse that struck the perfect note for dinner after work. As usual, she smelled like Dove soap, the kind my mother used when I was a girl.

Compared to Kevin, in my black slacks and yellow shirt, I looked like a bumblebee.

"What are you hearing at the paper about Green's prospects?" Kevin asked as we waited for our salads. "My patient numbers dwindle every week."

"The highway. The lake." I fidgeted with the cloth napkin in my lap. "Some people call it 'small-town syndrome.'"

"I think I've seen a case or two of that." Kevin attempted to smile, but it came across as sorrowful. "Daddy says it's like the dominoes started falling, and no one can stop them."

"Is the Lakeside Neighborhood Association doing anything?" I asked.

"Daddy's had several emergency meetings," Kevin said, "because so many of his members have gotten laid off."

"That group is fortunate to have Mr. Marcus," I said. "Your father not only has a vision but the heart to go with it."

"He's devoted to helping people in Green," she said. "Just like you are."

I guffawed and was grateful the room was empty, except for a waiter watching the sports channel behind the bar. "Not me," I said. "Your parents, Eva, Pastor Jean . . . they're the kind of people who make a difference."

"Oh, don't be silly," Kevin said, putting her hand on my arm. "You've changed Green for the better, and you know it."

My eyes felt moist. "I don't feel like I've done enough to keep downtown going," I said. "We didn't adequately analyze the impact of the highway. Or catch on to the salvinia problem at the lake."

"The paper does an amazing job with such a small staff," she said. "No one anticipated this crisis."

"Apparently Jerry did," I said. "He's strutting around town like the king of industry. I, on the other hand, try to keep my hair combed and ponder whether Eddie's red overalls will fade if I wash them with the towels."

She chuckled, a rich, comforting sound. "Welcome to my world," she said. "It'll get easier."

"Are you sure about that?"

"One-hundred percent," she said. "I can assure you from personal and professional experience. You're a great mom."

Eddie's little face popped into my mind. "Why doesn't anyone tell you how earth-shattering having a child really is?" I asked. "It changes everything. Every single thing."

"And yet you're still buying the Bayou Freez," she said. "Most new mothers wouldn't tackle that. I need to hear more about that decision."

"I don't want to buy it," I said, "but Chris and I can't bear to see it torn down. It seems like a symbol of all that's going on downtown." My eyes widened. "You like real estate. Do you want it?"

Kevin held her hand up like a stop sign. "Don't even suggest it. I haven't finished fixing up the rental property I already own. You've admitted downtown's drying up, and that old drive-in is a mess."

"But it's picturesque," I said. "And quirky. That building is one of a kind."

"Then it's a good thing you're buying it," Kevin said.

"Chris and I have our hands full and then some. Maybe someone else will step up."

Kevin picked up her fork, but didn't take a bite. "There's another challenge developing. I've been appointed committee chair to negotiate to keep the hospital open. In the middle of raising a son, trying to keep a romance going, and looking into sick kids' ears, I have corporate owners who want to shut it down."

My stomach flipped. "When did this happen?"

"The preliminary meeting was this morning," she said. "The patient census is low. The owners voted to close the ER, and they may downgrade the entire place to a clinic. They say Green's too small to sustain its own hospital."

I sighed. "Can't a woman even have a baby around here without the whole town falling apart? The *Item* should be on top of that story."

"You're too hard on yourself," Kevin said. "You can't have stories before they even happen."

"It's our responsibility to keep people informed," I said. "I'm not on top of things the way I was before Eddie was born."

She smiled.

"I'm serious," I wailed. "This is hard."

Kevin patted my hand across the table. "Let's quit talking business," she said. "I have something else to tell you, but it's not for publication."

"You know I don't like off-the-record," I said.

"Tough," she said, and continued. "Terrence and I are considering buying Major's development on the lake."

"You're buying a house in that neighborhood? I thought you hated Mossy Bend after all that trouble with Major's discrimination."

She smiled and wiggled her eyebrows. "Not *a* house. We're dealing on his development. Terrence wants to get into Bouef Parish real estate, too."

"But . . ." I wrinkled my nose. ". . . The lake's such a mess right now. Are you sure that's a smart deal?"

"That's precisely what makes it a great deal," she said. "It's dirt cheap."

"That's because the lake is full of dirt instead of water."

Kevin laughed. "Not forever. Terrence has done tons of research. The state has a plan to eradicate salvinia. The cold should kill it, and they can let the water back in."

"But that's not a guaranteed fix," I said. "Katy had that in her story last week. They've never had such a widespread, invasive weed before."

"Even so, they'll find a fix," she said. "It may take a while. People haven't given up on Bayou Lake property altogether."

I put my hand to my heart. "Does this mean marriage is on the horizon?"

"Now we get to the real reason you came to dinner tonight." She looked at her watch. "Fifteen minutes till you asked. You *are* losing your investigative touch."

I shrugged and grinned. "I like a million-dollar real estate deal as much as the next person, but I'm waiting to see the engagement ring."

"Be patient," she said. "We're moving forward, but I'm not ready."

"Terrence is a great guy," I said. "You love him. Marry him. I can testify that being married is wonderful."

"I'm not just getting a husband when I marry. Asa's getting a dad."

"Terrence will be a fantastic dad," I said. "Asa loves him, and he loves Asa."

"I pray about it every day. I'll know when the time is right." She reached for my menu, and I knew I'd matchmade as much as I could for tonight.

"Until then," I said, "maybe Terrence would like to buy the Bayou Freez."

"Nice try," Kevin said.

Voices behind me broke up our exchange, and I turned to see the manager ushering Zach Price and Katy to a table.

"Katy?" I said, shock making my voice reverberate across the room.

"Lois?" Katy said with a gulp. "Why aren't you home with Eddie and Chris?" She blushed as the words spurted out. "I mean, I didn't expect to see you here tonight."

I looked from her to Zach. "Apparently not," I said. "What's going on?"

Zach, never much for standing aside, strode to our table, scrutinizing Kevin for a second too long before speaking to me. "Your secretary told me you didn't do evening meetings."

"This isn't a meeting," I said and was aggravated that I'd defended myself. "And what about you?" I looked pointedly at Katy.

Zach scowled. "I invited Katy to tell me about her college journalism work. So where's that boy of yours that I keep hearing so much about?"

"Eddie's with his grandmother," I said. "I don't usually take evening appointments." *Or daytime appointments with you.*

"Eddie," he said slowly. "So you did name him after the managing editor in Dayton."

"Ed was a good man," I said. "And he *is* the reason I wound up moving to Green. Chris and I agree it's the perfect name."

Katy spoke up, her color still not right. "His middle name is Thomas, after the *News-Item*'s veteran copy editor. Tom's the guy who died trying to warn us about the tornado."

"He's named for two of the best journalists ever," I said. "Edward Thomas."

"You, too," Katy said. "Edward Thomas Craig. You're a great journalist, too."

"Are you buttering me up?" I asked, only half kidding.

"Maybe a little," she said, scooting away from me. "Hey, Dr. Kevin. How's little A.C.?"

That led to a round of awkward introductions, which carried us along for a couple of minutes. I used the time to attempt to figure out what Katy was doing with Zach. I could only pray this wasn't a date. Nevertheless, that meant it might be a job interview. I would wring Zach's neck before I'd let him take Katy away from the *Item*.

"Would you folks like to join us?" Kevin asked, while I fumed.

"We've got a table over here," Zach said. "Maybe some other time."

"I didn't realize you had joined the country club," I said, turning the statement into a question.

"The management's great to work with," Zach said, throwing a smile across the room at the lone waiter. "In a big city, you'd have to jump through all sorts of hoops, but it was easy as could be here. Oak Crest has allowed Post Media a temporary membership until we decide what our plans are."

Kevin's eyes met mine, and I knew we were both remembering our battle to get into the club a few years ago. "Easy as pie," Kevin said softly. "Welcome to Green."

Katy edged away from our table, and Zach gave two quick nods of his head, one to me, one to Kevin. "If you'll excuse us, I suppose we'd better be seated," he said.

"See you later, Lois, Kevin," Katy said, now practically trotting.

Settling two tables away, they ordered, ate, and chatted, while I strained to catch what they were saying.

"I've lost you for the evening, haven't I?" Kevin asked. "I knew you weren't listening when you didn't comment on my suggestion that we split the hot fudge brownie."

"I don't like it," I said. "Katy's too young for Zach, and I don't want her hanging around with him. He's digging for something. She's not used to dealing with corporate execs."

Laughter came from the table.

"Sounds like she's doing OK to me," Kevin said. "Now, are we having dessert or not?"

Zach pushed his chair back and started to stand, and I rose quickly. "I'm going to the restroom," I said. "If the waiter comes over, I'd love some of that brownie cake."

Trying to look nonchalant, I scurried to the vestibule behind Zach. When he came out of the men's room, I was sitting on an outdated velvet chair, pretending to listen to my voice mail.

"Hey, Lois," Zach said. "This place looks like something out of the past, doesn't it?" The big mirror was rimmed with the kind of lights found in a movie star's dressing room, and the carpet was a faded teal blue. The furniture looked like a living-room suite from someone's great-aunt's house.

But I hadn't staked out the men's room to discuss the hallway décor. "What are you up to?" I hissed.

"I like this place," he said. "It's old-fashioned. Like I told you, Katy and I are discussing the state of college journalism." He pulled a reporter's notebook out of his sports coat pocket and referred to it. "She's a bright young woman. Very ambitious. She reminds me of you in your younger days."

"You're taking notes?" I asked.

"I jotted a few ideas. I'll need them when you and I sit down to confer."

"I'm not conferring with you, Zach," I said. "I don't work for you anymore." A reporter's notebook in someone else's hands always made me nervous. Coupled with the idea of Zach cozying up to Katy, it made me downright anxious. I stood, knocking my purse off my lap. One of Eddie's pacifiers fell onto the carpet, and Zach picked it up.

"So, you're a working mother now," he said. "How things change."

"That's something we can agree on," I said. I thought of Ed and his plans to buy the *News-Item* and move to Green, about his death, my fight for the paper, falling in love with Chris. Eddie's birth. Seeing Zach triggered memories of my old life. It didn't make me miss it.

"Being a mother is the greatest job I ever had," I said. "Hardest, too."

"Even better than owning your own newspaper?"

"Owning the *Item* is great," I said, "but having a child . . . no comparison. Eddie and Chris are the best things that ever happened to me. How about you? You haven't remarried?"

"Nope." He gave a quick shake of his head, every hair in place. "With the corporate reorganization, I pretty much live out of a suitcase. Not much time for relationships."

"I still don't understand what brings you and your suitcase to Green," I said.

"I'm trying to keep my job," he said, "same as most people."

"But in Green?"

"It's part of a bigger plan," he said. "If this works out, I can swing a transfer."

"What kind of plan?"

Katy entered the small area. "Zach's company thinks consolidation will save small newspapers in dying towns," she said.

"Not exactly," Zach said. I could tell he didn't like Katy chiming in.

"But Green isn't dying," I said. "We're just going through a phase."

"That's what I told him," Katy said before moving through the heavy door into the ladies' room.

"It'll be all over town soon enough," he said. "This newspaper grant is a big deal nationally. It's unprofessional of you to refuse my efforts to set up an appointment to talk about it."

"I'll consider it," I said and returned to my table.

Zach pestered me by phone again the next morning. I agreed to meet him for lunch at the Cotton Boll Café. "I'm not going to help you beat my newspaper," I said, "but I'll meet with you if you'll quit calling."

"What can it hurt?" he asked. "We worked together for years, and you never know what might unfold."

"There's not enough money in Green for two newspapers," I said.

"Maybe not," he said, and I pictured his careless shrug. "But at least hear me out."

"I'll have to bring Eddie."

"Fine," he said.

When I got to my favorite lunch spot, ahead of Zach, a sign made out of a white paper take-out sack was taped to the door. "New Hours: Closed Tuesdays and Wednesdays until further notice."

Holding Eddie's carrier, I pressed my face against the smeared glass window and searched for a sign of life, startled when the owner, not wearing his usual uniform, opened the door. He held a dishtowel in his hands.

"We're shut down today, Miss Lois," he said, opening the door and gesturing for me to get Eddie out of the sun. "If you want chicken and dumplings, you'll have to come back Thursday."

"You only close on Thanksgiving and Christmas," I said, following him into the café, the fluorescent lights off and the French fry baskets empty.

The door opened as I spoke. "Sorry I'm late," Zach said, looking every inch the big-city journalist in his navy blazer and tan slacks with a blue-and-yellow striped tie.

"We have to find another lunch place," I said.

"Adjusting my hours," the owner apologized.

"Is your business hurting, too?" Zach asked. He barely acknowledged me and didn't even look at Eddie.

The owner wiped a smudge off the counter. "Matter of fact," he said, "business is mighty slow. Between the lake, and that new highway, and the heat, I'm thinking about taking my first vacation in years."

Zach introduced himself and pulled his familiar notebook and high-dollar ink pen out of his jacket pocket. "Mind if I ask you a couple of questions?"

"What about lunch?" I interjected.

"Name a spot, and I'll meet you there in ten minutes," Zach said.

We decided on a fish restaurant on the edge of town, and I hauled Eddie and my gear out to the SUV, wondering if I should have stayed to listen to the interview. Once I started the engine, I couldn't force myself to drive away. I looked back at the café, a staple in my daily life. I might have imagined the library or the bank cutting hours, but not the Cotton Boll.

A burst of energy shot through me as I looked up and down Main Street and glanced at Eddie in the rearview mirror. "Mommy's not going to let you down, Baby," I said, as I put the car into drive. "We'll find a way to save your hometown."

Zach arrived at the chain restaurant thirty minutes late. I'd already eaten a basket of hush puppies and had fed my son a messy dish of cereal.

"So, this is Eddie," Zach said, pulling out a chair and placing a file folder on the Formica surface.

"My son," I said as proudly as I'd once spoken of a story that had been a finalist for a big journalism prize.

Eddie, strapped into his carrier on the table, performed his trick of a real smile with a tiny spit bubble on the side of his mouth and then looked at Zach and laughed. I glowed. "How are your boys?" I asked.

"They're good. I don't see them as much as I'd like, but I talk to them almost every day."

"How do you do it? I couldn't leave Eddie like that." The words sounded harsh, and I hadn't meant for them to. "I mean, it must be so hard." I stroked Eddie's chubby leg, his delicate skin as soft as a petal on a rose.

"You do what you have to do," Zach said, clearing his throat and studying the menu. "I have to keep a roof over their heads."

"I suppose." I felt sorry for him for the first time and didn't like the way it made me feel. I acted as if I was looking at my menu, even though I'd decided twenty minutes ago what I wanted.

"I'm dying to know the truth about why Post Media and a journalism foundation are spending money to send you down here," I said.

He inspected the bright-yellow laminated menu as though it were a calculus textbook and spoke without looking up. "Corporate wants more market share. When Gina covered the tornado down here, she mentioned what a good operation you have in Green."

"Gina was covering the story of a lifetime," I said. "Those aren't ordinary in this little place."

Zach looked up and shrugged. "We have several papers in Louisiana, Texas, and Arkansas. We want to merge with a few more. We know you, and thought this would be a good place to start."

"The paper is not for sale," I said. "We've fought hard to hang onto it, and I'm not selling. Never. And I don't want to merge." Eddie's stomach made a funny gurgling sound, which ruined some of the firmness of my statement.

"If you ever decide to sell, let me know. Until then, we'll try to partner with you or run you out of business." He laughed as though he were joking, but I knew he wasn't. "One way or the other, Northwest Louisiana will be the hub for papers in the three-state area. This is an innovative plan, and Post will use the grant to make it work. You can be part of us or fight us. Your choice."

"Most papers are pulling back on state coverage," I said. "There can't be much readership down here. Couldn't you pick another *regional hub?*"

"You've said yourself there are fascinating stories here," he said, lowering his voice as the server approached.

"The *Item's* coverage interests people in Green," I said after ordering, "but I can't imagine readers in Shreveport or Lafayette or over in Dallas being all that interested."

"This can further your career," he said. "You'll get all sorts of national attention."

"We've had plenty of national attention," I said. "The tornado brought enough people to town for a journalism convention."

"You thrive on this sort of thing, Lois," he said. "I've seen you in action."

"No, Zach, I thrive on keeping my newspaper afloat, helping my employees, loving my family, and trying to keep this town from becoming a statistic. Please move this idea to some other lucky editor's town."

He snorted and sipped his iced tea, making a face. "How much sugar do they put in this stuff?" he asked and called loudly for the waitress. I looked down, wishing I'd met him in my office. I didn't want people to think we were friends.

"This tastes like cough syrup," he said to the middle-aged woman. "Give me a glass of water. No ice."

I tried to catch her eye and offered what I hoped was an apologetic look. Then I sucked in my breath and plunged ahead. "You've never gotten over the fact that I quit in Dayton, have you? You want to make me pay for not taking that job you found me in Ashville."

"That's ridiculous," he said, not acknowledging the server when she set a glass of water on the table. I was pleased to see it filled with crushed ice.

"The wire services are reporting that Post is up for sale," I said. "Is this some last-ditch effort to save your career?"

"Rumors come and go," he said. "I'd rather talk about working out a deal with the *News-Item*." He picked at a hush puppy as though he'd never seen one before. "We're not enemies, Lois. We're colleagues."

Zach spoke softly to Eddie, making the baby laugh, before looking straight into my eyes. "Help me out here. It could be what you need during this transition in Green."

All of a sudden it was all too much. The paper. The baby. The lake. The highway. "I'll consider what you've said. That's the best I can give you for now," I said, gulping my tea.

"I'm at the Lakeside Motel," he said. "You have my number."

"Surely you don't mean you're staying in Green?" I asked.

"This is not a small project, Lois. It's gaining momentum. Besides, the Lakeside Motel is a lot better than one of those chains in the suburbs of Chicago or Des Moines. I'm staying here as long as I can."

"Oh, the expense account," I said. "That's one thing I gave up when I bought the *Item*."

Zach gave a small smile. "I thought owners got all the perks."

"That's only true when your paper makes money," I said. "Despite what Post Media thinks, advertisers aren't exactly plentiful around here."

"You need the corporate approach," he said. "Trim the fat."

"You have to have fat before you can trim it."

"I know how to handle these tight economies," he said, "and I'll work them step by step. I need someone to coordinate our bureau here. Then I'll move on to another hub. Hopefully by then I'll have convinced you to merge with us."

My eyes narrowed, and I slapped my hand down on the table. "So that's what the dinner with Katy was about," I said. "College journalism programs! Right! Well, good luck with that. She's mine."

A quick thought hit me as I voiced the words. Katy wasn't really *mine*, even though I'd lured her into the world of journalism. She was a strong-willed young woman who would make up her own mind.

"Perhaps," Zach said. "She hasn't agreed to come to work for me."

Thank goodness.

"But she hasn't turned me down either," he said. "I think you're overlooking obvious areas in which we can partner. There will be market overlap."

"We don't do things in Green like we did them in Dayton."

"Maybe a fresh approach would help both of us," he said. "How's your lunch?"

As we settled into our meal, Zach steered the conversation to chitchat, and I followed with relief. We talked about people we knew in the business, one of those perpetual "follow-the-dotted-line" conversations that journalists love, then to television shows and college football prospects.

"I e-mailed my kids photos of cypress trees near the motel this morning," Zach said. "They've never seen Spanish moss before and think it looks like a monster."

"Those trees are gorgeous," I said. "In the fall, they're a rusty-red color. In spring they are light green."

"Will the weeds in the lake kill them?" he asked.

"We don't think so," I said, "but no one's sure yet. Some people say we'll have to cut some of the trees. This is a situation that won't be fixed quickly."

"The Lakeside owners told me their business has dried up as fast as the lake has."

"I've heard," I said. "They don't deserve that. The Taylors are some of the finest people I've ever met. Kevin, my friend you met at the club last night, is their daughter."

"They're proud of her," he said. "They told me all about how she adopted a son and how his other grandfather died in the tornado."

"Papa Levi," I said. "I don't think Kevin or her parents have gotten over that yet."

Zach hemmed and hawed, in very uncharacteristic Zach style, and I wondered if he was stumbling over how to express his sorrow. "What about your other friend? Does Becca date anyone?"

"Zach," I warned. "You're not going to be around long enough to start a relationship. Becca's got a lot to handle."

"Going out a few times wouldn't be a big deal."

"Leave Becca and Katy alone," I said. "Please leave all of us alone."

"You act like you want to live in a bubble," he said.

Eddie babbled all of a sudden, as though part of the conversation. I turned to soothe him and thought about what Zach was saying. *I did want to live in a bubble—one that didn't include corporations trying to run my town.*

"He's a happy boy," Zach said. He stood abruptly, volunteered to pay, and almost rushed to the cash register. Watching him sign a credit-card receipt, I had a twinge of satisfaction that my former employer had bought me lunch.

As I reached for the baby carrier, I saw a newspaper clipping peeking out of his file folder lying on the table. "Mayor Details Travel Expenses," the headline read, and I recognized it instantly as the piece we'd done in response to complaints about Eva's trip to Florida.

"You have to watch out for journalists," I said in a soft voice to Eddie. "You never know what they're up to."

When I drove back from lunch, I noticed Katy sitting on a bench by the lake. She looked small and young, the way she had when I first saw her hanging around the newspaper's loading dock. At least her hair was a normal color today. "I really don't have time for this, Eddie," I said, looking at my son in the rearview mirror. "But I have to make time, don't I?" He slept on, and I sighed and wheeled into the parking area.

"You following me?" Katy asked as I walked up, Eddie in his stroller. She gave a small smile to the baby, but it didn't seem to make its way up to her eyes.

"Yes," I said. "My private eye has the day off, so I'm tailing you myself."

She gave a half-hearted laugh and watched while I situated Eddie in the shade and draped a tentlike blanket over his stroller for extra protection. "It's kind of weird watching you take care of a baby," she said.

"Eddie does require lots of attention," I said, sitting next to her. "But I'm still the same person. I just travel a bit heavier."

"He's adorable," she said softly, leaning over. "Everything seems to be going good in your life."

"We're blessed, that's for sure," I said, trying to determine where she was headed. "But everyone has their challenges."

"I guess . . ." she sighed.

"What's wrong, Katy?" I asked, putting my hand on her arm, much as I might have on Eddie's. "I haven't seen this look on your face in a long time."

"Do you think I have talent, Lois?"

Of all the questions I might have expected, that was not one of them. "Of course I do. I tell you that all the time."

"Zach says that you don't appreciate me enough. He says that a college student with my skills should be making more money."

"He's probably right," I said, "but no one at the *Item* is getting rich."

"He offered me a job," she said, "with more money and benefits. He wants me to use what you've taught me to help drive you out of business."

"I see."

"I wouldn't do that for all the money in the world," Katy said.

"I know you wouldn't."

"Being a grown-up is harder than I thought it'd be," she said. "There are so many decisions to make. Maybe I should have gone to New York this summer after all."

"I'm sure glad you didn't."

"For real?"

"Oh, very much for real," I said. "You're a tremendous help at a time when I have too many plates spinning in the air."

"Zach says his company has deep pockets. He's adamant that if you don't cooperate with them, they'll run you out of business."

"They'll see pretty fast that the flow of money in this town is about like the flow of water in that lake right there," I said.

"I like working at the *Item*," Katy said. "I want a life like you have—one where you enjoy your job and try new things."

Once more her words surprised me. "I haven't thought about it like that," I said. "But I love my work. I love my life, for that matter. Whatever you do in the future, I want the same for you."

"The first thing I'm going to do is come up with better ideas than Post Media ever dreamed of," Katy said.

"I like the sound of that."

Dub stopped by our house the middle of the next week with a load of mulch for our flowerbeds.

"You didn't have to do that," I said. "You've already done more than your share in this yard."

"Think of it as a gift for Aunt Helen," he said. "She'd like what you and Chris are doing with her old place."

Smiling as I remembered my friend and mentor, I followed Dub to his truck, baby monitor in one hand and Holly Beth in the other.

"The bark will keep your plants from getting quite so dry in this weather," he said.

"You don't trust me to water them, do you?"

He chuckled and gave an ecstatic Holly a scratch on her stomach. "After we went to so much effort to get things to grow, I don't want to lose them in this heat."

"You're turning into a regular farmer," I said.

"Joe's taught me a lot," he said. "His garden produces more tomatoes and okra than I'd have thought. He's a heck of a businessman."

"Is he planning to keep living with you?" An immigrant, Joe Sepulvado had moved in with Dub after the tornado crushed his trailer, killed his wife, and seriously injured him.

"For now," he said. "He thought he'd go back to Mexico where his grown kids are, but he's unsure since Maria and her boys have come into his life."

"Are they officially a couple?" I loved the thought of a match between the young woman Chris had given his mobile home to and the farmer unfairly accused of setting fire to the newspaper.

"Looks that way, although Joe says he's too old for her."

"Maria's not a child," I said. "She can see what a good guy he is."

"Eva and I sure enjoy his company," Dub said. "He keeps an eye on my house when I'm out of town and has been teaching her Spanish."

"Are you gone a lot?" I asked, feeling slightly guilty since the question went beyond chitchat.

"Off and on," he said. "I'm checking on investment opportunities that might help Green."

"I thought you retired," I said.

"There's only so much golf you can play. I even shot a round with that friend of yours from up North this week."

"You golfed with Zach?" That twosome concerned me.

"He's aggressive," Dub said, unloading the mulch like a much younger man. "He hinted about me putting up capital for a project his company's got going. They're using some sort of journalism grant as seed money."

"And were you hooked?" I asked.

He shook his head. "I'm more interested in businesses with local leadership."

Brushing the dirt off his hands, he headed for the truck. "If I were you, I'd keep an eye on Zach Price, though. He seemed awfully chummy with a lot of the guys at the club."

8

A member of the Daffodils and Daisies Garden Club has received a written reprimand for not wearing green during the club's citywide flower tour. "Everyone knows that green makes me looks pale," Theresa Montgomery said in her appeal to the club president. "I had a green outfit made for my dachhsund, Sassy, for the event and had her nails painted green. The club's actions are unfair." The president disagrees, saying, "The rules are clearly stated when you join."

—*The Green News-Item*

Three people responded to my Friday editorial to save the Bayou Freez, not exactly a groundswell of support with less than a week left before demolition.

One reader suggested the building be turned into a car wash, another advocated tearing it down to build a strip mall, and the third wanted the paper to donate it to the nearby Baptist church.

"We can't donate it," I explained to the caller. "The newspaper doesn't own the property. We're trying to find a buyer." *Or there goes Eddie's college fund . . .*

The idea of a church taking over the building seemed to have merit, though, and I put Eddie in his stroller and zoomed down to Becca's flower shop to talk about it.

"I'll be with you in a second," she called from the back, little bells jingling as I maneuvered the gargantuan stroller through the door. The smell of fresh flowers hung in the air, mixed with potpourri and the scent of a lemon candle.

Becca stepped through the curtain that separated the retail space from her workroom, an orange kalanchoe in her arms. "I read your editorial. Did you find a buyer for the Bayou Freez?" she asked, leaning over to smile at Eddie in the process.

I shook my head somberly. "For some reason," I said, "no one is all that interested in a rundown building in a declining area. Even if it does have character and a great view."

"It's such a shame," she said. "Restoring that building could change the whole personality of downtown. If I weren't so in debt, I'd buy it. We'd have milkshakes in every flavor and those big, juicy hot dogs."

I could almost see the little stand bustling with business as she spoke. "That's a great dream," I said. "What a wonderful spot that would be . . . but we're out of time, and there aren't any lookers. The best suggestion so far is to call the downtown pastors to see if they're interested."

Becca set the plant on a primitive table with peeling blue paint. "I tried that," she said. "I spoke with both the Methodists and Baptists last week. Their offerings are down so much that they're not undertaking any capital projects. They're concerned about paying the electricity bill and making payroll."

"You contacted them?" I was surprised and impressed.

Becca looked apologetic. "I wasn't trying to butt in, but I know how much you have going on. I also e-mailed the gardening club and most of the civic clubs."

"That's great," I said. The oddest feeling of pride and jealousy zipped through me. "Any possibilities?"

"Everyone loves the idea of you and Chris buying it." She looked sheepish. "I guess it's always easier when other people solve our problems, isn't it?"

"Apparently so," I said dryly.

"Almost everyone says the same thing," Becca said. "'You can count on Lois. She'll figure something out.'"

My heart swelled for a second, replaced by reality. "See this little guy," I patted Eddie's head. "He's more work than a full-time job, and I also happen to have one of those."

"Think how much fun it'll be to fix the Bayou Freez up," she said. "I'll be happy to help. Others will, too."

It did not escape me that she was now speaking as though Chris and I were the new owners. Looking around her shop —which had merchandise, personality, and no customers—I nodded. Becca had already figured out where I stood on the Bayou Freez. "If we have to, we'll buy it," I said. "But absolutely only as a last resort."

"I understand," she said. "But I want our children to have places like that." She looked at Eddie, who seemed to take everything in. "I don't want Cass and Eddie's world to be one big chain store."

"Nor do I," I said. "Nor do I."

Becca knelt again to speak to Eddie, who let out a string of unseemly noises right as she got at eye level. "Glad to see me, huh?" she teased.

"Eddie!" I scolded, as though he could understand what sounds were appropriate in public.

Becca gave her light laugh and motioned me to the back. "Sounds like he might need changing. You're lucky you get to take him to work with you. With Cassie in preschool, I miss her so much."

Lifting Eddie out of the stroller, I followed Becca into the back as she held the curtain aside. The room looked like a cottage in a design magazine. Tall black containers of irises, tulips, baby's breath, and roses lined one old wooden table, next to a deep sink and a jumble of baskets and vases. Rolls of ribbon wound around a wooden dowel, and a series of floral sketches in colored pencil were tacked to a bulletin board, alongside copies of the most recent obituary pages from the *News-Item* with funeral service times circled.

Light streamed in from a row of high glass-brick windows, and the back door was propped open, an oscillating fan on the counter blowing the hot June air around. "You've created the perfect design studio," I said. "Every time I walk back here, I relax."

"I need to hear that today," she said, her face flushing. "That pipe sprang a leak and made quite a mess." She pointed underneath the sink where water dripped at a steady pace into a plastic bucket. "I don't want to spend the money, but I guess I'll have to get a plumber."

As she talked, she pulled out a towel and folded it on the countertop. "There," she said. "The perfect changing station."

She reached for Eddie. "Let me change him for you. It's been a while, but they say you never lose the knack."

She hummed as she removed the dirty diaper, Eddie waving his hands and blowing bubbles.

"You really have a way with children," I said. "I still feel like I'm practicing."

"You're a great mom," she said.

"I'm a control freak," I said, "and with a baby I feel like I'm always out of control." I picked up the discarded diaper and sealed it in a plastic bag. "My life revolves around things like poopy diapers."

"You'll figure out what you can control and what you can't," she said. "Before long, everything will be second nature. You won't even remember what it was like before you had Eddie."

"It already feels like that," I admitted, noticing a photograph of a child taped over the wall-mounted telephone. "Is that your daughter?"

"That's my girl," she said. "Cassandra Marie. That's her very first school picture. She was so delighted that she got to wear her favorite red shirt. Little things make her so happy."

I looked more closely, captivated by the little girl's sweet smile.

"Cassie is darling in every way," Becca said. "She has Down's syndrome."

"Oh, I'm sorry." I regretted the words the second they left my mouth. "What a terrible thing for me to say. She's a beautiful little girl."

"She's the biggest gift I've ever been given. The two of us make quite a pair."

"You're single, right?" I halted.

Becca jiggled Eddie up and down in her arms, his eyes heavy with sleep. "I've never been married," she said. "I made a few colossal mistakes a few years back. But I don't consider Cassie one of those. I thank God every day for the chance to be her mama."

"Do you date?" I asked.

She laughed and shook her head. "That newspaper friend of yours asked me the same question when he stopped by the store yesterday."

"Zach came in here?"

"He tried to act like he was interested in my business, but I think he was more interested in my love life."

"He's got children," I blurted out.

"And I've got a daughter," she said. "That won't keep me from dating someone, but I'm not ready to move on when it comes to romance. Besides, who has time? Right?"

The sound of running water punctuated her words, and I ran over to where the bucket under the pipe had overflowed. "You don't need a date," I said. "You need a plumber."

I grabbed a nearby bowl and slid it under the leak. Hefting the bucket, I went to the back door, trying not to slosh water onto the floor.

"I'll empty this in the alley," I said, "and see if we can figure out a way to patch that." The sunshine warmed my face as I stepped outside, and I blinked as I adjusted to the light.

"Lois?" a man's voice said a few feet away. "Can I help you with that?"

Placing the bucket on the pavement, I shielded my eyes and looked up to see Lee Hicks putting a ladder in the back of a construction truck. "Becca's got a plumbing issue," I said. "Her drain has come loose or something."

"I can take a look at it, if she wants me to," Lee said. "I just finished up a repair job for the drugstore, and I'm running a few minutes ahead."

"She'd appreciate it," I said, making a muddy mess as I emptied the bucket. "The problem is getting worse in a hurry."

Lee stepped into the back of the shop on my heels, his face lighting up as he saw Eddie, who was back in his carrier on the counter. Becca was on her knees putting duct tape on the pipe.

"This is a disaster," she said when I drew near, rocking back on her heels in a position that would have pulled every muscle in my body.

"We probably need to turn the water off," Lee said.

Becca froze, like a squirrel I'd once seen nearly grabbed by a hawk. "What are you doing in here?" she asked, her manner not quite what I'd expected.

"I ran into Lee in the alley, and he offered to help," I said. "He knows how to fix things."

"That's not the way I remember it," Becca said, and went back to taping the drain.

"That's not going to work," Lee said. "You can't patch that."

"Tell me about it," the florist mumbled.

I gingerly put my hand on Becca's shoulder. "Why don't you let Lee try?"

The atmosphere was so charged that I thought my hair might stand on end, but Becca nodded and scooted over.

Lee squatted on the floor and examined the pipe. "At least this is something I can fix," he said, glancing at Becca. "Let's put the bucket back while I grab a few tools."

"I don't need any help," she said, but her words lacked the bite they had earlier.

"It's not a big deal," Lee said, looking into her face with something akin to pure longing. "I'll be right back."

As he exited, Becca exhaled and slumped against the counter where Eddie lay.

"I know you might not be all that fond of Lee, but he's very handy," I said.

"I shouldn't let him darken the door," she said.

"So it was that bad?"

"I'm sure you've heard the gossip." She pulled out another old towel and wiped up puddles on the floor. "Lee Roy dated me before he got into so much trouble."

"Was it serious?" I looked toward the door, relieved that he hadn't returned.

"I thought so," she said. "But apparently his wife wasn't that keen on the idea."

Lee Hicks had not stepped foot in the *News-Item* since the day he was arrested for stealing from the paper, so I was surprised when Tammy told me he was in the lobby.

"Why didn't you send him in?" I asked. Tammy rarely announced anyone, and usually it was when an unwelcome guest appeared.

"He said he'd rather not," she said. "I'll watch Eddie while you talk to him."

Lee was staring at a framed copy of a front page, holding his work cap with both hands and shifting from foot to foot. When I moved through the swinging gate into the foyer, he jumped at the squeak. "I could squirt some grease on that thing for you," he said. "It's been making noise for years now."

"This place has more problems than Stan can keep up with," I said.

"I wasn't being critical." He almost wrung his hat inside out. "You've got a nice newspaper plant here."

"Thanks," I said, touched. "Would you like me to show you around? We've made a lot of improvements since you left."

"I'd better not," he said and twisted the hat again. "I didn't expect to feel so weird walking through that door."

"I felt the same way when I visited the Dayton newsroom," I said. "Even after working there so many years, it felt odd."

"At least you didn't leave there in handcuffs," he said. "I didn't depart under ideal circumstances." He took a deep breath. "That's what I need to talk with you about."

"Why don't we sit down in the newsroom?" I said. "We'll have privacy in there."

"If you're sure," he said. "I don't want to cause any more trouble."

"This is no trouble," I said and led the way.

When we entered the room, he gazed around like a person visiting the house he grew up in after years away. "Looks about the same," he said after a few seconds. "Smells the same, too. Microwave popcorn."

"The food of choice around here." I poured each of us a cup of coffee, mostly to give myself something to do. "Why don't you have a seat and tell me why you look so worried?"

He perched on the edge of an ancient settee and grimaced after tasting the coffee. "Another thing that hasn't changed," he said. "No offense, but this stuff tastes terrible."

"That's the same pot, and it still burns the coffee." I pointed to the small refrigerator that sat in the postage-stamp-size break area. "There's probably some of the same food in the fridge, too."

He laughed and nodded at Holly's cushion, his shoulders seeming to relax. "You've added a dog bed since I was here."

"That's where Queen Holly Beth stays when she's not with Estelle and Hugh—or you," I said. "She tolerates Eddie, but she keeps her distance." I hesitated. "Sort of like Becca did with you earlier today."

He sipped the coffee again. "I need to discuss that with you."

"You don't owe me an explanation," I said. "That's between you and her."

"You and Chris have been good to me, and I respect you," he said. "I don't want to leave unfinished business out there. I've asked God for forgiveness, but I need to make up for what I've done. I'm going to do whatever I can to help others learn about Christ's love." He looked over at me as intently as Pastor Jean giving a benediction. "I mean that, Lois."

I uttered a silent prayer of thanks and hope as I thought of Becca and what the unfinished business might be. Iris Jo and Pastor Jean and my husband were much better at these conversations than I was.

"I ran around on my wife," Lee blurted out, looking into the souvenir coffee mug that Tammy had brought back from her honeymoon in the Caribbean. "I lied to Becca. I told her I was getting a divorce."

"I thought you were divorced," I said.

"That came later," he said, "and I don't blame Sheila—my ex-wife—at all. She moved on with her life. Not only was I cheating on her, I was stealing from you."

He shook his head. "Lois, I did so many things wrong that I can't count them all. I want to make everything right, but it feels like trying to push a rock uphill . . . Not that I'm making excuses. I want to fix things."

"What's done is done," I said. "You can't go back."

"I don't want to go back," Lee said. "I want to repair the damage that exists because of me and go forward."

"Have you straightened things out with Sheila?" This had to be one of the strangest discussions I'd ever had in Green, and I'd had some doozies.

"We made amends while I was in jail. She's remarried and moved to Hattiesburg. She forgave me but would never have taken me back." He winced. "Not that I blame her. Her new husband seems like a nice guy, treats her right."

"And Becca?" I asked.

"I hurt her badly," he said. "She was naive in many ways, and good-hearted. Everything I wasn't."

He got up and walked over to the composing room area, idly rubbing the drafting table surface, still smeared with wax from years before.

"Do you know about Becca's brother, Barry?" he asked.

"She mentioned that he had an accident and lives with her mother. That's about all."

"I met Becca through Barry when he worked as a handyman for Major." Lee looked at me with his piercing eyes. "Major got Barry mixed up in some bad stuff."

"What kind of bad stuff?" I wished I could pick up a notebook without stopping his flow of words.

"Drugs, I think." He ran his fingers inside the neck of his shirt. "It had something to do with cooking meth. Selling it."

"Are you sure, Lee? Major's done a lot of things in his day, but that doesn't sound like him."

Lee exhaled. "I was never able to prove it, but I suspect he had Barry and another guy do the dirty work. Word was that he ran the business out of his real estate office. They even had a drop spot somewhere downtown."

"And now?" I was almost afraid to ask this question.

"Barry's been clean since his accident," he said. "I heard Major got out of the business when he went to jail."

"What kind of accident did Barry have?"

"The two of us were riding motorcycles, and he lost control. His bike slid off the road one way and he flew the other way." Lee seemed to be back on that day as he recounted the accident.

"Are you sure you want to tell me this?"

"I have to," he said. "I love Becca, and I want to be there for her and Barry. I don't have any hope that she'll get back with me, but there has to be something I can do. Maybe you can help me get through to her."

"Becca and I haven't been friends for all that long," I said, wishing Tammy would bring Eddie in or that the phone would ring. "I didn't even know until recently that Becca had a daughter."

His coffee sloshed over the side of his cup before he righted it.

"Becca has a child?"

"I'm sorry," I said. "I assumed you knew."

He shook his head as though his head were too heavy for his neck. "She deserved to meet someone after the way I messed with her. She's a special lady."

9

Fred Robertson says it's "bye, bye birdie" at his house and is looking for a home for a pair of parakeets he bought his wife, Margie, for Mother's Day. "She says it's hard enough to pick up after me without having to clean up all those seeds." The cage and other accessories will be thrown in, so give Fred a call if you're interested.

—The Green News-Item

Chris got out of the SUV with the willingness of Holly Beth going to the vet.

"How did I let you drag me into this?" he asked.

"It can't hurt to look," I said. "Besides, if we don't save it, who will?"

"Eddie, let me tell you something," Chris said as he situated our son in the stroller. "Your mother cannot be reasoned with. The best thing is to go with the flow."

I grinned. "Don't fill his head with the wrong idea." I looked into our little boy's eyes. "Eddie, there's always a lot going on in Green."

"There's always a lot going on when you're involved." Chris gave me a quick kiss. "Now remember, we're just looking."

"Lead the way," I said, amazed at how laidback my husband was. He did let me get us into peculiar situations.

Chris pulled the key to the Bayou Freez out of his jeans pocket and turned on a high-voltage smile. That smile told me he didn't care what I got into, he'd be there with me.

Bayou Lake, with little water, had the bright green glow of Louisiana summer. That was how the town got its name, or so the legend went. The smell of cut grass drifted over from the thick, old church lawn.

As we walked underneath a live oak, children's voices sounded from the park across the street. The thick glass bricks on the side of the drive-in shimmered. I closed my eyes for a second.

As I breathed in a feeling I couldn't quite identify, Eddie said, "Ma-ma."

My eyes met Chris's. "Did you hear that?" I asked. "He said 'Mama.' "

"I told you he would talk before long," Chris said, grinning as if he'd just won a championship football game.

Kneeling by the stroller, he said, "Could you say 'Mama' again by any chance? You've made your mother a very happy woman."

"Ma-ma." Discovering the new sound delighted Eddie, and he laughed and then said it again, laughed and said it again. "Ma-ma."

We all three laughed together.

"I can't wait to tell Iris," I said. "Ellie's been jabbering a lot longer than Eddie."

"She's a month older than Eddie," Chris said. "You know Kevin told you not to compare them."

"Ma-ma," Eddie said.

"I'll never compare them again," I said and walked toward the side of the Bayou Freez, a big smile on my face, Eddie laughing and patting the bar on his stroller. "I knew he was going to like this place."

As it turned out, the key wasn't needed. The padlock at the side of the building had been broken, and the door swung open with a creak, revealing an old-fashioned kitchen with stainless steel counters and a huge turquoise freezer. A leak stained the ceiling tile. Paint peeled from humidity and age, and the faucet on the deep sink was rusted, one of the spigots tilted at an alarming angle.

A stack of bar stools with shiny red vinyl covers were jumbled in the corner.

"I can't believe those things are still in here," Chris said, maneuvering the stroller across the room. "These used to sit outside at the counter. I wonder if I can find the one I scratched my name on."

I covered Eddie's ears. "Eddie'll be grounded if he does that," I said. "Don't give him any ideas."

"All the kids did it," Chris said, untangling one from the pile. "Well, I'll be." He paused. "There's Fran's name."

Always taken aback at hearing the name of Chris's first wife, who had died of breast cancer, I looked down at Eddie and swallowed hard. If life had worked out differently, Eddie would have belonged to Fran and Chris. I would be hunkered down in a Midwestern newsroom, working every holiday and trying to convince myself I was happy.

"Mommy loves you so much," I said to Eddie, overwhelmed.

"Ma-ma," he said, smiling with a hint of slobber.

My heart expanded.

Chris set the stool down and pulled me into the crook of one arm, pushing the stroller with the other. "Let's see what kind of shape the outside tables are in."

The front of the small building was covered with a large portico, with a flagstone patio, unusual for North Louisiana.

The tables and benches were concrete, covered with bright mosaic tiles, a few of which had been broken or marked on. The front of the building was glass, with two serving windows, and the faded menu, also covered in graffiti, offered a litany of milk shake flavors and ice cream options.

Standing under the cover, near the window, with the weedy lake in sight, I felt removed from the rush of daily life. "This place is a treasure," I said. "Becca was right."

"It feels exactly the way I remember it . . . minus the milkshakes," Chris said.

I absorbed every detail and felt an unexpected excitement. I tried to tamp the feeling down by remembering the pile of bills waiting on my desk, the committee work I was behind on at church, and our late-night play dates with Eddie. But I knew the idea seed had sprouted.

"Let's talk about it some more," I said.

Chris shook his head. "Every time you suggest we talk about something in that tone of voice, I get roped into one of your schemes."

"You never get roped into anything you don't really want to do," I said. "Don't you think it might be fun to own this place?"

"Sure," he said. "I also would like to own a convertible, a party barge, and a vacation home in Montana."

"Look at that lake," I said. Even with the heavy growth on the lake bed, the view was still inviting. "What a location!"

"We could just have a picnic in the park across the street," he said. "It'd be a lot cheaper."

"I know it sounds crazy," I said. "But I don't like what's happening to our town. If someone doesn't do something, Eddie won't have much of a future here."

"We both work, and we have a baby," Chris said. "Has that possibly slipped your mind?"

"We don't know how long the school will stay open," I said. "This could be your fall-back career."

"Selling ice cream?"

I smiled. Nodded. Tried not to laugh. When he said it, it did sound ridiculous.

"How could we possibly renovate this old place, and who would run it?" he asked. He, too, was trying not to laugh. Maybe we were both slightly hysterical.

"We'd have to work out the details. I lined up financing on the paper, so I'm sure we can figure out something."

"Didn't you say Dub's looking for local investments?" Chris asked.

"He barely mentioned that," I said.

"You could give him a call," Chris said. "I must admit owning the Freez could be interesting."

Chris and I were good for each other. And, unless I was mistaken, we were buying the Bayou Freez.

Our banker, Duke, wore a bemused look when we signed the papers for the loan ten days later. Chris and I looked stunned, Dub pleased, and Major was triumphant.

"I thought you two were bluffing," Major said to Chris and me. "But darn if you didn't go through with it."

"I thought we were bluffing, too," Chris said and squeezed my hand affectionately.

"It'll be wonderful," I said, stepping away from Major. Even though my staff had yet to confirm Lee's allegations about drug deals, I didn't doubt they would.

"I'll get my things out of there this afternoon, and it's all yours," Major said.

"You said you didn't have anything in there," I said, annoyed and suspicious. "You sat on that property for twenty years. It's ours now."

Major squirmed in his chair and then stood. "I didn't want to admit it," he said, "but I want to take one more walk through for old time's sake. Surely you can't fault me for that."

Chris threw me a quizzical look. "We aren't going to start cleaning it up until this weekend, anyway. I suppose it'll be all right."

"I'll leave everything as I found it," Major said and walked away before I could respond.

Chris gave Dub, who had co-signed for our loan, a hearty handshake and strolled over to visit with Duke. Dub walked over to me and nodded as though I'd done something special. "Miss Lois, this is exactly what downtown Green needs," he said. "Towns all over the country will want to copy the Bayou Freez."

"I hope you're right, since you put your money behind it," I said. "You invested in the future of Green. Not everyone would do that."

He gave a small shrug, looking very courtly in his suit and tie. "I'm making up for bad decisions I made in the past. I can't change what happened, but I can do better from now on."

The sentiment reminded me of a sermon Pastor Jean had preached not long ago. Putting the past behind us, we have to move forward. Press on, she'd said, to do what we're called to do.

Dub interrupted my thoughts. "Combine old-fashioned business like the ice-cream stand with modern conveniences. That'll be a powerful mixture."

For a second, I could see the line of people of all ages waiting for their ice cream, Eddie and Ellie playing nearby. *Could this be one of those callings Jean taught about?*

Unfortunately, that lofty notion didn't last long. As the day wore on, the fog of doubt seeped in. Eddie was fretful, and the more he whined, the more nervous I got about running a new business. The picture of flying banners clashed with aching feet and too little sleep.

After Chris came by to take Eddie home, I felt lonely. I was driving myself crazy.

Tammy calmed me, which on any other day would have worried me even more. "What's the worst that can happen?" she asked when I settled at my desk.

"We go bankrupt," I said.

"I thought Major gave you a good deal," she said.

"The price seemed good at the moment, but we don't have a ton of savings, and now we're in debt to the bank, and Dub. What if this was foolish?" I put my face in my hands.

"Look at these pictures, and you'll know you did the right thing." She spread a row of eight-by-ten black-and-white photographs on my desk. We were poring over them when Katy strolled in.

"Well?" she asked. "Did you go through with it?"

"You are in the presence of Lois Barker Craig, newspaper owner and ice-cream mogul," Tammy said. "Come see these pictures I found in the storage closet."

A row of 1950s cars, with long bodies and big fins, were angled in the parking lot at the old drive-in. Stylish teens lounged at the stools lining the side counter, some of their clothes not all that different from what Katy, Molly, and their friends wore.

In one picture, a cluster of children hunched over a table, each of their tongues licking big ice cream cones. Another showed a group of workmen, wearing khakis and shirts with their names embroidered over the pockets, backed up to the wall. They held large paper cups with straws.

"Life seemed simpler in those days," I said.

"Who says you can't create those feelings again?" Tammy asked, picking up a photograph and studying it. "The sale of the Bayou Freez is already bringing back memories. People are talking about it all over town."

"That place is going to be so much fun," Katy said. "I want to hang out there."

"There's a paintbrush with your name on it," I said.

All three of us picked up photos and studied them.

"Can we do a photo layout?" Katy asked. "Ask readers to send in their Bayou Freez memories?"

"What a great idea!" Tammy said.

There it was again, that hint that I was called to do this. Could owning an ice cream stand make a difference? "I wish every decision could be crystal clear," I muttered.

"Isn't that the truth?" Katy said. "You're not nervous, are you?"

"A little torn," I said.

"That's natural," Tammy said, as though she bought and sold buildings every day. "We flip out when we take a risk, but it's an adventure."

"Are you mocking me?" I peered at her.

"I'm congratulating you," she said. "Let's start fixing that joint up."

While the rest of the world relied on e-mail and other forms of social media, Green remained attached to the phone-tree. One person called another who called another until whatever announcement, prayer request, or committee assignment spread through Bouef Parish.

With Tammy's enthusiasm and Iris Jo's organizational skills, the calls resulted in what looked like half of Green showing up for the unofficial "Bayou Freez Work Day Extraordinaire," so-named by Katy.

On this early July Saturday, Chris, Eddie, and I walked from the parking lot at the newspaper, leaving the handful of parking spaces for volunteers. I hoped some would show up.

"This place is awesome!" Katy said.

"It's really cool," Molly said, pulling poster board and markers out of the trunk of her mammoth-mobile, Anthony climbing out of the passenger's side with his crutches.

"How're you doing?" Chris asked his former basketball player.

"Still working out, Coach," Anthony said, holding up a crutch. "If I keep up my therapy, they'll let me throw these things away by the end of the year. I can't do any hard stuff, but I'm good with a paintbrush."

"This is the best summer ever," Molly said, draping one arm around Anthony's waist and the other across her best friend's shoulder.

She and Katy, as different in appearance as two young women could be, wore homemade white T-shirts sporting red lettering that said, "Shake, rattle and roll" and a drawing of a red cup holding a milkshake.

"We're going to get this place going," Katy said. "Remember when you talked us into selling snow cones that first summer you were here?"

I smiled, thinking how long ago that seemed. Katy, who had lost her boyfriend Matt in a car accident, had hung around outside the newspaper with Molly, a shy, studious African American girl. As their friendship blossomed, they helped with everything from raising money during the first Homemade Ice Cream Social to working at the paper.

They've grown up, I thought as I watched them flit around our new building.

By lunchtime, we'd hauled off two loads of trash, washed all the windows, and updated our work list. Walt had three freezers of homemade ice cream under way, and Stan grilled hot dogs, while workers scraped, swept, straightened, and reminisced about their teen-age days at the drive-in.

"Your friend Zach called me again last night," Katy said as she scrubbed the outside counter.

"What?" I said. "I thought you turned him down."

"For a job, yes. This time he asked me out on a date."

"That's creepy," I said.

Katy agreed. "I don't trust him."

"Why not?" Tammy asked, shooting before and after photos as we worked.

"Zach is one of these people who tells you what you want to hear," Katy said. "He tried to lure me to work for Post, and I see him around town with Mr. Jerry and that crowd. Now he's all flirty with me."

"Is it true he's putting pressure on the paper so we'll have to merge or something?" Tammy asked.

My eyebrows rose. "I've told you all I know about his plans. I quit keeping secrets from my staff a long time ago."

She shrugged. "Everywhere I go on assignment, Zach's there. He's a little too chummy with the good old boy's club, if you ask me."

"When I refused his job offer, he said it didn't matter," Katy said. "He says the *Item* will beg him for help by the time this is all over."

"Post Media won't stick with this project," I said. "They hit and run on efforts like this."

"Maybe," Katy said. "Zach also asked me how to reach Alex. He'd like to bring him back to Green to be Post's regional reporter. That grant funding would pay a year's salary."

"The *News-Item*'s got history here," I said. "Zach's starting from scratch, and that doesn't work in Green." The vision of Zach constantly working behind my back made me nervous, but I didn't want to upset my employee-owners. Hiding my anxiety wasn't the same as keeping a secret.

"Would Alex be interested in coming back?" Tammy asked.

"Maybe," Katy said. "But he likes living out West."

"Have you two broken up for good?" Tammy asked.

"More or less," Katy said. "He acts so wise and important with his reporting job, always cutting me off to do this interview or go to that meeting."

She made a small huffing noise. "A few weeks ago he told me I didn't understand what it was like to hold down a job. I reminded him that I've worked at the *News-Item* since I was sixteen. I know what a job looks like."

She jabbed at the air with her finger as she talked. "He's not even twenty-five," she said. "Can you imagine what he'll be like when he's thirty?" The way she said it, thirty was somewhere a few moments ahead of retirement.

"I wish there was someone around here," she said and wandered off to talk to the young preacher, who was pulling up weeds behind the building.

At dark, our helpers were still there. I savored the enthusiasm and hard work of friends and family, who almost made me forget my reluctance to buy the drive-in. After sandwiches for supper, a group of women and a handful of children gravitated to lawn chairs. We chatted with the mood of an old-fashioned summer evening, talking and laughing.

Ellie was passed from person to person, and Iris laughingly picked up her pacifier off the ground, wiped it on her pants, and stuck it back in Ellie's mouth.

"Are you sure that's sanitary?" I asked, reluctantly handing Eddie to Pearl Taylor, one of the few people who passed my baby-watching standards.

"She probably gets more dirt than that playing in the yard with Stan," Iris said.

"Don't you worry about her getting sick?"

"Oh, Lois, you know I do, but I try to relax and enjoy her." She looked over at Katy, who was talking to a group of students from Grace Chapel. "When Matt died, I didn't think I'd ever get to be a mom again." Reaching for her daughter, she snuggled Ellie up against her, inhaling. "I regret how much time I wasted on things that didn't matter."

"But babies are so helpless." I picked up Ellie's chubby hand. "I'm scared something could happen."

"We're up to the challenge." Iris's sweet smile lit her face. "I promised the good Lord I would not miss a moment of joy if I had another chance after Matt died."

"Keep reminding me to chill out. Because I want to do everything right with Eddie."

My mother-in-law walked up at the end of our conversation and chuckled. "There's no such thing as a perfect mother," she said. "You'll feel a lot better when you realize that."

"How can you say that?" I asked. "You're the perfect mom."

Estelle looked at the group. "Isn't she the sweetest daughter-in-law?"

"She doesn't strike me as sweet," Tammy said.

"Having children keeps you humble," Kevin said, pointing to where Asa played under the watchful eye of Terrence. As we looked at the boy, he scratched his behind and stuck his finger in his nose.

Maria, a friend from the Spanish ministry at Grace, looked at her three boys playing nearby. "Children grow up so fast," she said in her lilting accent. "So many good people help me, or I would be very nervous."

The group turned to see Joe Sepulvado pick up the smallest of the trio and brush him off when he stumbled. Maria smiled. "Like Joe. He's kind."

"Handsome, too," Tammy said.

Maria blushed.

"Tammy," I scolded and met Maria's gaze. "So, are you serious?"

The group of women laughed. "You promised Chris no matchmaking," Kevin said.

"I'm not matchmaking," I protested. "I'm trying to stay up on the news."

We laughed again.

"So, Kevin, what about you and that hunky lawyer from Alexandria?" Tammy asked.

"Terrence and I are taking it slow and easy." She turned to Pearl. "And, Mama, don't you say a word."

Pearl put on the glasses she wore on a chain around her neck and stared at her daughter. "I don't know why my baby girl can't find it in her heart to marry that man," she said. "I never thought it would take her this many years to find a husband."

"I like being close to my mother and father, even if they do meddle," Kevin said with a smile. "I'm not ready to move to Alexandria."

"Terrence could commute like I do," Tammy said but gave an uncharacteristic sigh. "It is hard living and working in two different towns, though."

Becca, carrying a bouquet of daisies and wild grasses in an old soda-fountain glass, walked up at that moment.

"Do you find it hard?" Tammy continued, as though Becca had been there for the entire discussion.

"We're talking about children, marriage, and commuting," I said, smiling at the flowers, my friends murmuring compliments as the conversation swirled.

This kind of visit was one of the things I enjoyed most in my life in Green, threads of advice and encouragement, people drifting in and out, paying attention even as they fussed over a child or helped with a chore.

"It's not so bad except that I miss my daughter. She's in preschool, and my mother keeps her when I'm at the shop," Becca said. "I only drive about forty-five minutes each way."

"So you and your husband live in Ashland?" Tammy asked.

"I'm not married," Becca said and looked down. "I'd better get going. I wanted to drop those flowers off before I head home. Let me know how I can help when you start remodeling."

Satisfied that Eddie was content in Pearl's arms, I impulsively grabbed Becca's hand as she moved from the group. "Let me show you what we've done so far."

Her stiff posture relaxed a fraction. "Thanks for saving the Freez, Lois. To me, this offers a lot of hope for the future of downtown."

"You helped us decide," I said.

"It's going to be a perfect community gathering spot," she said. "It's come alive, and you haven't opened yet."

I steered her to the side door. "Our business plan leaves a lot to the imagination. If Dub hadn't wanted to save this from the wrecking ball, we'd have never gotten that loan."

"That would have been a shame," she said, gazing up at the tiled roof.

As I moved into the kitchen, a rat, my least favorite of creatures, scurried behind the refrigerator, and I jumped back with a yelp. Becca waved her hand and brushed past me. "It's only a mouse," she said. "Every old building has them."

"It looked like a rat to me," I said.

A peal of laughter came from her, a sound I'd never heard Becca utter. "You're the bravest woman I've ever met," she said. "Surely you aren't bothered by a mouse."

"Rat," I said. "You didn't get as good a look as I did." Staying as far as possible from the last place I'd seen the rodent, I showed Becca the outdated kitchen.

"So will you restore it to like it was in the good old days?" she asked.

"We hope to make it what it was when Chris was in high school. Then we can only pray that'll draw people back downtown."

"It has so much potential," she said, rubbing her hand across the stainless steel counter.

Hearing a rustling noise behind the appliances, I grimaced. "Potential for what, though?"

"I'm happy it didn't get torn down," Becca said.

"I am, too." Inwardly I was praying for wisdom. This had been my first prayer in Green, and I found myself uttering it now on a daily basis.

10

Henrietta Gray and Dorothy Gibson have put together a "Read on the Road" trip for next spring to acquaint library patrons with literary landmarks. "We've rented a bus and will travel to places that were important to some of our favorite Southern authors," Hen said, adding that they also will seek out diners they've seen on television.

—The Green News-Item

Katy's crush on our young preacher and any remaining interest in Alex decreased when she met the guy who could be "the love of her life" online.

"Oh, Lois," she gushed in the newsroom one afternoon in late July. "I think he's the one for me. He's cute and funny and an awesome guitar player. You should see his music videos."

Exhausted from a long night with Eddie, who had a summer cold and cried when I put him down, I rolled my eyes.

"What's wrong with that?" Katy wailed. "Why can't you be happy for me?"

"Katy," I sighed, "you've never even met this guy. He could be an eighty-five-year-old man with no teeth for all you know. One of your college friends might be playing a prank on you."

"Lois, you don't understand modern dating." By the way she spoke, I could have been a Tyrannosaurus Rex. "Couples meet online all the time. Don't you remember that secretary from the high school? She moved to Michigan and is ecstatic."

Katy held up her hand before I could respond. "Colt is going to be famous," she said. "He's getting airtime on radio stations around Albuquerque, and that's only the beginning for a musician."

"Maybe people do meet online all the time," I said, "but how can you be sure this guy is who he says he is?"

"Intuition," she said. "He's a great writer. Besides, I've checked him out. I do Internet research all the time for work and school. I've seen pictures, too."

I rubbed my neck and said a silent prayer for patience. "How'd you happen to connect with him?"

She gave another of her dramatic sighs. "You are so out of the loop since you had Eddie," she said, looking over her shoulder at the crib. "No offense, little guy."

Eddie kept right on playing with a rubber toy.

"Katy, you told me not two weeks ago that you're too young to get tied down," I said. "But now you're in love with Pony or whatever this fellow's name is?"

"Colt," she said. "You know it's not Pony. You never take me seriously."

"Katy," I said, not wanting the conversation to escalate. "You're a smart, cute woman. You are an outstanding journalist and have inspired me almost from the day we met. I worry about you getting personal with someone you don't know."

She moved from her usual spot propped against my desk to one of the chairs. "I'm not stupid," she said, drawing *stupid* into two very long, loud syllables. "I haven't told him where I live or anything like that." Slowly she calmed down. "Besides, he's told me all about his parents. They're from Houston and have a ton of money. He can have any girl he wants."

"Then why is he trolling around online?" I asked, trying to keep the bite out of my voice.

"Because he's tired of the girls he meets," she said. "They don't understand how creative he is."

Only through the force of will did I keep from rolling my eyes again. "Katy, what about Alex?"

"I don't know . . . I do like Alex. You know that. He's really a good journalist, even though I get mad at him sometimes. But he's far away."

"But you text and talk nearly every day. Isn't that better than e-mailing some guy you don't know?"

She grumbled but semi-agreed. "Alex has been great to me. He's taught me a lot about reporting." She paused, and I knew that look. Katy was trying to decide how much to say.

"And?" I prompted.

"Alex helped me when I wanted to leave school and move home last year," she said.

Stunned by this revelation, I dared not say a word too soon.

"I was worried about my parents, and Molly did all that statewide stuff to help the school." She shrugged. "I felt left out, and I wanted to come back to Green."

"But?"

Katy gave a half-chuckle, half-groan. "You're not going to let me slide on this, are you?"

I waited.

"Alex told me I needed to get my degree, and I didn't have to be in the middle of everything here. He said he misses y'all, too, but we have to grow up. The move was good for him, and going to college in Georgia is good for me." She brushed her hands against each other. "So there."

"Sounds like Alex has a little more sense than I gave him credit for," I said with a smile. The young reporter flashed into mind, heading into the paper in ragged tennis shoes and dirty jeans. He had the tenacity of Holly Beth with her rope toy when he went after an investigative story. And the energy of Chris's high school athletes.

Katy rubbed the toe of her leather flip-flop against the floor. "I wish he hadn't moved so far away."

"Aren't there any guys around here you might like? I thought you and Luke were getting close."

"Luke's kind of boring," she said. "He never wants to go out or anything. He says we have to be careful not to give people the wrong idea."

My opinion of the handsome young pastor went up a notch.

"What does Molly think about all this?" I asked.

"She doesn't get it," Katy said. "She's been dating Anthony for nearly two years, and they're like an old married couple. She doesn't look at other guys."

"Molly's always respected you," I said. "She has good judgment."

"In most things," Katy bounced up on the chair. "But she didn't go off to college, and her perspective is limited."

"She marched on the state capitol to save Green's schools," I said, my voice dry as a Louisiana field in July. "That doesn't seem all that limited to me."

"That was fantastic," Katy said, her voice rising on the last word, "but she's a homebody. She doesn't think much of online dating."

"Maybe it's the mom in me, but I worry about this." I tried to give my voice a playful note. "Will you be extra careful for my sake?"

She smiled, a vestige of a younger Katy looking back at me. "Sure, Lois," she said. "I promise you're going to like Colt when you meet him."

"Maybe *you* should meet him first," I said.

On one end of my worry spectrum was Katy. On the other was Eva, who continued to come under attack by a small group of vocal Jerry Turner supporters. The ripple effect of the innuendos had turned into what Aunt Helen would have called "a fine mess."

When the mayor stopped by my office with her hair windblown and a coffee stain on her blouse, I knew something was up. "I apologize for not making an appointment," she said, "but I need your feedback."

She carried Sugar Marie in her arms, and Holly Beth jumped up and down like a kangaroo when she saw the two of them. Eva put her dog on the floor and fawned over Holly before detouring to sneak a peek at Eddie and Ellie, in the middle of afternoon naps.

"They don't have a care in the world," she said. "Why do we let our lives get so harried?"

"Are you OK?" I asked.

"I'm good." She smiled. "But I find my patience is a lot thinner than it was when I entered office." She sat in one of my office chairs, her knees together, her back straight and stiff.

"I'm sorting out my future in politics," she said. "I intend to run for Congress. Jerry plans to run for mayor, and he'd like to make me appear weak. He's using a collection of circumstantial evidence to make me look guilty of wrongdoing. Politics have gotten so nasty that I'm wondering if they're worth it."

"Don't even think that," I said. "Green needs you now more than ever." Pushing my chair back, I moved into the seat next to her. "I suppose you've heard the new round of rumors?"

Jerry had returned to my office the day before with his campaign manager, who happened to be the guy who would gain the most from the proposed industrial park.

"You mean the stories that I stymied efforts to clean up the lake? Yes, I've heard those—and just about anything else you can dream up."

I snorted. "If people put such imagination to good use, no telling what we could do in this town."

"That posse of Jerry's follows me to every public appearance. They're requesting all manner of city records." She fingered the topaz ring on her right hand, a gift from Dub after she'd led the tornado recovery efforts. "Apparently he's convinced your friend Zach that a big expose would help Post get support from the business community."

"Jerry's posse needs to spend its energy on improving things," I said, "instead of tearing buildings and people down."

"It's tedious." Eva gave a small laugh. "But it's the democratic process. When people are involved, it tends to complicate things."

I threw her a knowing look. "It's the same way with readers. They drive me crazy, but they're the reason I do what I do."

"That's one of the many things I admire about you, Lois. You say what's on your mind."

"So do you, Mayor. It's one of the attributes I try to copy."

"You care more about Green than citizens who have lived here for years," she said. "That first afternoon you walked into my office, I realized you'd make a difference here. When I heard you were buying the Bayou Freez, I knew that downtown would make it. And it won't be an industrial park that changes it."

Studying my clasped hands, I considered her words.

"I thank God every day for bringing me here," I said at last, meeting her eyes. "Even on the darkest days—and we've had our share of those—I've known deep down this is where I'm supposed to be."

"That's the way I feel about public office," Eva said. "Being mayor tangles up my personal life at times, but I believe I've been called to serve."

Sugar Marie and Holly Beth got up from the towel where they'd been lying and raced around the room, hurling themselves into Eva's lap. If they'd been children, I was certain they'd be giggling.The mayor gathered them close, stroking their fur. Both dogs closed their eyes and wagged their tails.

"This is just the visit I needed," Eva said.

"You won a tough mayoral campaign, battled the board of directors at the country club, saw us through unspeakable tragedy, and kept your ex-husband from closing the schools. I know you'll make a great congresswoman."

She held both dogs as she stood. A lesser woman would have looked like Aunt Bea from Mayberry, but she looked stately.

"I'm not going to be deterred by a smear campaign," she said. And I knew she meant it.

11

The sheriff's department was called to The Shiner Marina on Black Bayou after two brothers got into a fight over a good fishing spot. "Roger Leachman was annoyed with his brother, Barry, for sharing a prime bass-fishing location with a neighbor and launched Barry's boat with no one in it." The sheriff also reminds you to wear a life jacket and not to litter.

—The Green News-Item

The brochure for the conference in San Diego enticed me with its catchy seminars and hotel amenities. Mayor Eva coaxed me to go, bringing the materials to my office and mounting a persuasive campaign.

"I'd go with you, Lois, but with the trouble with Jerry . . . Not even dinner at the White House would get me out of town. Look at the courses they're offering, though. The top tourism and marketing experts in the country will be there."

I flipped through the four-color booklet, entitled "Small Towns, Big Dreams." My eyes lingered on the photograph of a woman in a luxurious white spa robe, gazing out at the ocean, not a wrinkle or diaper in sight. I savored the description of an optional outing to Coronado Island.

"You'll come back with all sorts of good ideas," Eva cajoled. "The Green Forward Group has money set aside for continuing education, and I'd be more than happy to pay the balance—out of my own pocket, of course." She grinned, looking younger and more relaxed than she had in months.

"I enjoy workshops," I said, studying the list of restaurants in the resort. "And downtown definitely needs a boost." The walking tour of antique stores, with pastries and gourmet coffee, made my heart speed up, and I laid the brochure down, smiling. "But I'm not about to go off and leave Eddie. Maybe next year."

Eva seemed momentarily taken aback and then smiled. "Chris Craig is a lucky man," she said.

"Not half as lucky as I am." I couldn't say it or think it enough.

The conference wouldn't work for me, but I had a better idea and sweated my way down to Becca's shop to discuss it.

She balked when I broached the subject of the conference.

"Oh, I couldn't do that," she said, running her hand over the smooth surface of the brochure as we stood in her workroom.

She studied the paperwork. "There's actually a session called 'Don't Let Customers Bypass Downtown.'" Her voice held the note I got when the *Item* broke a big news story. "There's so much to learn."

"You might not want to go without Cassie," I said. "But if you could get away, the Mayor and I think you'd bring a lot back from this."

"California." A world of longing filled the word as she uttered it. "I've never even flown before. There's no way I can afford this. You know how bad business is."

"Your expenses will be paid, and Eva offered to loan you one of her store clerks while you're gone. All you have to do is bring back ideas."

"I'm not sure." She hesitated, studying the brochure. "These people will be so smart. I barely got out of high school."

"You have your own business in a tough economy," I said. "That's an accomplishment most people can't claim. Especially not at your age."

"I want to do it," she said. "I'll talk it over with Grandma and see if my mother can help with Cass." Becca did a funny little hop, the way people who win new cars on game shows do. "This really is going to happen, isn't it? I've never had an opportunity like this."

When she returned from the West Coast, Becca and I had lunch at the Cotton Boll, which had cut its hours ever further.

"Lois, you can't imagine what other small towns are doing," she said. "The participants were super nice! Everyone took me under their wing." She opened her eyes wide. "One of the speakers even asked me out on a date."

"Did you go?" I asked.

"Of course not! He was way out of my league."

"Becca," I said, "no one is out of your league."

She wrinkled her nose. "I'm perky," she said. "Not pretty. Perky. Besides, I'm not interested in dating, not since Lee . . ." Sadness touched her eyes and then disappeared. "Still, it was nice being invited, and best of all, I got so many ideas for Green Forward."

Her words tumbled out so quickly I could scarcely understand her.

"No town is doing one thing that Green can't do," she said. "I thought other places had magic plans or something, but they're ordinary people like us."

"What do we need to do?" Her enthusiasm thrilled me.

"We're on the right track with Green Forward," she said, "and everyone was impressed with the Bayou Freez. They say a little spot like that can help turn downtown around. They call it an anchor."

She caught her breath. "I told them they should get you to speak at one of their meetings, since you're the one with the best ideas." Leaning forward, as though she had a secret, she continued, "All we have to do is come up with special events and spread the word outside of Green. We need to make people *want* to come to Green."

"Sending Becca to San Diego may have been the best investment we ever made," Eva said at the Green Forward follow-up meeting.

"You're a peach, Becca," the leader of the South Green Merchants Group agreed. "I appreciate the ideas to bring traffic to our area."

"The booklet on building antique traffic is outstanding," Rose said. "The Holey Moley can work with the Bayou Freez to turn downtown around. Shops like mine draw people off the highway."

"I haven't seen this sort of energy since Lois got us started," Pastor Mali from the Methodist church said.

"Everyone is so quick to jump on this silly bandwagon," Jerry complained. "These ideas cost money, and there are gaps bigger than the potholes on Route Two. Everyone in this room knows we don't have money for a marketing campaign." He turned to the pharmacist from down the street. "I don't know about you, but I'm not standing out on the highway holding up a sign."

A few people laughed at his joke, while Eva clenched her jaw and Becca winced.

"Unless . . ." Jerry stopped after the one word.

Uh-oh. Every time he did that, he was about to suggest something I didn't care for.

"Go on, Jerry," Eva urged. "Tell us what great plan you've come up with."

"Miss Lois here could swallow her pride and partner with that national news chain," he said. "They could tell people all over the country about Green."

I gritted my teeth, every eye in the room staring right at me.

"After all," Jerry continued, "if you hadn't bought the Bayou Freez, we'd be breaking ground for a new industrial park on that property. Seems to me if you really cared about Green, you'd not balk at Post Media's innovative ideas."

Surely steam was coming out of my ears by now. I could feel my face flushing. Maybe I was proud, but I didn't want to share any part of my newspaper with Zach and his corporation.

"Do you think Post could help us?" Becca asked, so much hope in her voice that I couldn't say no.

"I'll see what I can do," I muttered, my teeth still clenched.

I reached Zach in Baton Rouge, where he was meeting with a group of state legislators. Standing at the kitchen sink, I looked out at our chicken coop while we talked.

"Jerry said I might hear from you," Zach said, speaking in a whisper. "Should I expect the roof to cave in?"

I gripped the phone until my knuckles were white. "What would it take for Post to take Green on as a project?"

"You know what we want," he said. "Post wants to be full partners with *The Green News-Item*. It will help both of us."

"No," I said. "Forget it."

"What about saving downtown?" he said. "You need capital, and we've got that. We need local credibility, and you've got that."

"Let's start smaller and see what happens. Would Post do a co-op deal?" I swallowed hard, hating to make the next offer. "Maybe share regional advertising and coverage?"

"I'm open to talking about it," he said. "But only as a foot in the door."

I started to hang up, but recalled the empty parking spots on Main Street, the stagnant lake, and the lack of other prospects. "Come by my office when you get back to Green," I said. "We can work out the specifics then."

Male voices talked loudly in the background. "I've got to go now, Lois," Zach said. "The governor just got here."

Eddie started crying from his playpen. "So do I," I said.

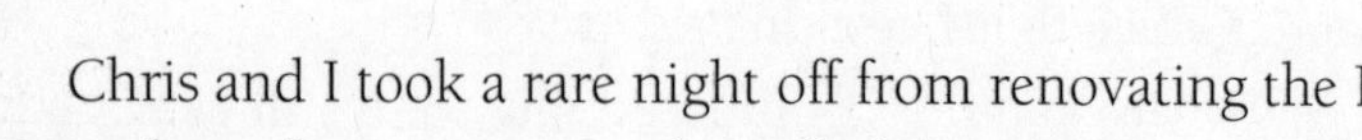

Chris and I took a rare night off from renovating the Bayou Freez later that evening and strolled down Route Two, Eddie cooing while we talked.

"Do you regret not going to the town conference?" Chris asked as I recounted the details of the Green Forward meeting and my call to Zach.

"Not in the least," I said. "Becca came back with great ideas, and I got to stay right here with you and Eddie. It all worked out."

Chris wore an old T-shirt with a cartoon catfish on it, salvaged from his parents' house after the tornado. In the twilight, it had an odd shine to it, and it reminded me of a dolphin statue in Becca's conference brochure.

Tilting my head, I studied it more closely.

"What?" Chris asked, looking down. "Did Eddie spit up on me again?"

"No." An idea was taking shape in my mind.

He tugged the hem of the shirt out of his shorts and turned it up to inspect. "Is it catsup?" he asked. "I thought I dropped some at supper, but I didn't see where it went."

I laughed and studied his shirt. "Have you ever seen those outside sculptures in big cities?" I asked.

Chris quit looking at the shirt and squinted his eyes. "Sculptures?" he said the word as though he'd never heard it before.

"Outdoor art," I said. "Like those cows they had in Chicago one time."

His head moved up and down, and I could almost see the simultaneous movement of his mind. It was clear he thought I'd lost mine."I saw horses like that one time," he said. "I think it was in Amarillo, Texas."

"What about catfish?" I asked.

"No," he said. "I'm pretty sure they were horses." He grimaced. "Oh, no. Not that look. Please, dear Lord, not that look."

"What?"

"Every time you get that look in your eyes, we wind up in the middle of something. Please, Lois." His voice had a half-playful, half-pleading tone.

"Why couldn't we have fish around downtown Green? Big, colorful fish, painted by local people?"

"You hated my catfish collection," he said, putting his hand across his heart as though I'd cut him to the quick. "Now you want a public fish display?"

"It'd be unique," I said.

"I'll give you that," he replied, and it sounded like Eddie laughed.

Surprisingly, Tammy thought the fish were a great idea. Katy and Molly groaned, throwing out words like *embarrassing*, *hillbilly*, and *laughingstock*.

"You don't get out of Green enough," Katy said. "You and Chris need a vacation. Really. I'm serious."

"The fish could be fun," Iris Jo, always our peacemaker, said. "Businesses could sponsor them, and the *News-Item* could organize a contest to choose designs."

"I wonder if there'd be a zoning issue," Linda, all reporter, said.

"One way to find out," I said. "Eddie and I are going to see the mayor."

"You'll be able to reel Eva in," Tammy said with a smirk. I winced and pretended I hadn't noticed.

Eva's response fell somewhere between Katy's and Iris Jo's. "It's different," she said, lingering over the word *different*. "Done right, they could be eye-catching." By the look on her face, I assumed she was picturing what they might look like if done wrong.

"We could use them to stir up regional publicity," I said. "They'd give people another reason to come downtown."

"It's a risk," Eva said. "A creative risk, but a risk nonetheless. Green businessmen aren't exactly the artsy type."

"It's not fine art," I said. "It's funky. It reflects Green's personality." I considered for a moment and plunged ahead. "I've agreed to talk to Zach about a partnership. Post might sponsor a sculpture, or help in other ways."

"Fair enough," Eva said. "If he takes the bait, I'll present the idea to the city council."

"Not you, too," I said.

I expected to get tired of fish jokes pretty fast, but I was taken with my idea. Maybe I had been in Green too long.

Energized by Becca's report and the public art idea, I stopped at her shop the next day. She was working on flowers in the back.

"What great ideas have you come up with today?" I asked. "And do any of them involve milkshakes?"

"I wanted to talk to you about that!" she exclaimed, her cheeks glowing. "Let's weave Green's comeback weekend into the reopening of the Bayou Freez."

She attached pink ribbon to a giant mum with a smile made out of pipe cleaners. "I've made an entire notebook of other possibilities. I've got . . ." She leaned over the spiral-bound book. ". . . Forty-seven ideas already."

I sat down on one of two wobbly stools at the battered worktable, pushing Eddie's stroller back and forth while I skimmed Becca's ideas. "A classic car show is perfect," I said. "Imagine vintage cars lined up at the Bayou Freez. It'll look like the old pictures Tammy dug out."

"We close off Main Street and let car clubs from all over the region display them and award a prize," she said, climbing up on the stool next to me. "Stores decorate their windows." She clapped her hands. "We can have a sock hop with old music."

Watching Becca was like seeing one of her flowers burst open. I leaned over and gave her a big hug, the kind I'd learned when I moved to Green. "You are such a blessing," I said.

Her eyes sparkled when she pulled back. "That's the nicest thing anyone's ever said to me."

"You're enthusiastic when everyone else is scared," I said. "Your shop is an original, even when business is slow."

"It's all thanks to you," she said. "You inspired me with the newspaper, and you weren't afraid to buy the Bayou Freez. Now you're talking about public art. Imagine that! Public art in Green."

"You do realize we're talking about fish sculptures," I said. "This won't be the Louvre or anything."

She giggled. A giggle from Becca. That alone was worth some ribbing about fish art.

I turned back to her spiral notebook. "Well, then." I tried for a brisk tone. "Let's see what other great suggestions we've come up with."

She pointed to a row of words written in purple ink. "We can hang a banner over Main Street. Or have a downtown antique show and flea market."

I read her big printed words. " 'Movie Under the Moon' would be fun, and a citywide picnic at the lake could be a great draw, but we might need to wait until the lake has water in it," I said.

We were hunched over the worktable when someone tapped on the back door, and it swung open.

Lee Hicks stepped in. "I was next door and wanted to make sure the patch job on the plumbing held up." He looked past us to the sink. "Any more leaks?"

Becca closed the notebook and stood up so fast the light-weight stool came up off the floor, almost tipping over. "The part you brought did the trick," she said. "It's good. Thanks."

As she talked, her voice was completely different from our chat moments ago. Lee straightened the stool, then lifted it, laid it on the table, and tightened one of the legs.

"A little wood glue would help here," he said. "I have some in the truck."

"That's OK," Becca objected. "I'll fix it later. I don't want to hold you up."

"It's not a problem," Lee said in a gruff voice. "I want to help you."

"I don't need your help," she said in a soft voice. "I'm making it fine on my own."

Sitting on the stool between them, I felt like a child who'd been put in the corner. I practically held my breath.

"Lois told me what's going on with you," Lee said.

I did?

Becca put her hand to her chest, as though she might be having a heart attack. "What did Lois tell you?"

"I know you've found someone else," he said. "I'm happy for you."

"You don't sound happy," she said. They seemed to have forgotten I was there. I was glad I'd left Eddie with Iris.

"I'll never forgive myself for hurting you," Lee said, leaning against the table, hands outstretched, palms up. "I'm thankful you have someone else in your life and hope he's good to you and your little girl."

Becca leaned back against the table, the two still flanking me. "Lois may have misled you," she said.

I had?

"I haven't dated anyone since you and I broke up," she continued.

Lee put his hands in his pockets and looked past me at Becca. "But Lois told me you have a child, a little girl."

Becca's gulp could be heard over the soft whir of the flower cooler. A truck beeped in the alley, and time seemed to have stopped in the workroom. "Cassie is a very special child," she said.

"I saw her picture the other day," Lee said, pointing to the bulletin board. "She's a beautiful little girl."

Becca closed her eyes and drew a deep breath.

"She's your daughter," she said.

I knocked over the rickety stool I was sitting on.

12

The Meals Delivery program at First Presbyterian Church is looking for a new volunteer driver to replace Kathleen Wilson, who retired on her seventy-fifth birthday after twenty years of delivering lunches to area shut-ins. When asked why she was so faithful all those years, Kathleen said, "I hope someone will do that for me if I get old and need it."

—The Green News-Item

Scraping petrified gum from tables at the Bayou Freez, I watched Chris on a ladder, through the window. Eddie played with a mobile over his carrier on the counter, and I smiled as my husband dismounted, tickled our son, and climbed back up the ladder.

Our remodeling progress was slow, but after renovating the house on Route Two, we hadn't expected it to go quickly.

Unable to resist the lure of the two people I loved most in the world, I laid my work gloves on the table and went into the kitchen. "This is sort of fun, isn't it?" I asked, and Chris, his head in the attic, made a muffled response that I couldn't understand.

While I liked a good, solid plan in life, the Bayou Freez was all seat-of-the-pants. We'd bought it after little thought, a lot of prayer, and a few conversations. The remodeling was done by whoever showed up to help at night and on weekends. We debated daily whether this would be a year-round business or seasonal, but we had pretty much decided to replicate the Bayou Freez tradition in downtown Green as closely as possible.

We didn't know who would run it, and our opening date was as cloudy as the lake had been before the state drained it. My dream was to open for business by late summer, but Chris said we'd be doing good to have it open by next spring. "It's a bigger project than everyone thinks," he said.

One of the many things I loved about my husband was that he didn't rub it in when he was right. I had to be big enough to admit he was usually right.

Taking two steps down the ladder, Chris shook his head. "You can't believe how hot it is up there. Tell me again how you talked me into this?"

I opened an ice chest from home, pulled out a bottle of cold water, and extended my arm. "My irresistible charm and astute business sense, along with my urge to stick my nose into everything."

"Is that the same thing that got me into a massive home renovation project?" he asked, wiping sweat from his forehead with a faded bandana like his father used. "Because I doubt our sanity at the moment."

I opened a bottle of water for me and held it against my hot face, its condensation dripping down my chin.

"Think of how much fun this will be in the future," I said. "Eddie will be the coolest kid in town because he gets all the free ice cream he wants."

"Maybe we could just buy him ice cream at the grocery store, like normal people."

"You love this place." I hoisted myself onto the counter, sitting next to Eddie. "I can tell by the way you look at it."

"I'm never sure which of us is crazier anymore," Chris said, gulping the rest of his water.

"You have the same look in your eyes you had when you and I started dating," I said.

He threw back his head and laughed, and Eddie laughed, too, as though he were in on the joke.

"You're a lot better-looking than this place," Chris said. He climbed down the ladder, put his hands on my shoulder, and popped the strap of my white overalls, my after-work uniform for more than two years now. The T-shirt underneath had the sleeves cut out. My ponytail was in disarray, and I could feel stray hairs floating around my face.

"I'm a mess," I said.

"You're my kind of mess," he said as he laid a deep kiss on my mouth.

"Wow!" Katy's voice said. "I didn't know carpentry could be so romantic."

Chris turned slowly. "With my wife, everything's romantic," he said and started back up the ladder. "Glad you made it."

She stood in the doorway with Molly, young Pastor Luke, and Anthony, on his crutches behind them. "Reinforcements have arrived," Katy said.

"Put us to work," Molly said.

My questioning look roamed from them to Chris.

"Chris called us today," Anthony said. "He wants to open by Labor Day weekend."

"Anthony," Katy squealed, "it was supposed to be a surprise."

I looked back up at Chris, who still stood on the ladder, his head just beneath the ceiling, and he winked. "You had your heart set on opening this summer," he said. "A winter grand opening didn't sound that great for ice cream sales."

"You said there was no way we could get it open this year," I said.

"I've learned not to put anything past Lois Barker Craig," he said. "I figured, why not give it a try?"

"Coach says Green High teams don't know what they're missing," Anthony said. "The Bayou Freez was the hangout after every home game when he was a kid."

"Don't make it sound like that was a century or so ago." Chris's voice could barely be heard from where he worked. "Lois, assign these kids something to do."

"We're not kids," Katy protested. "Besides, we brought experts, so you'd better treat us with a little respect."

Chris stuck his head out once more, looking at a parade of volunteers pulling into the parking lot. Dub, Joe Sepulvado, and Maria piled out of Dub's pickup, and Iris and Stan got out of their big blue truck, going through the now familiar process of getting a baby and carrier out of the backseat.

"We owe a lot of people free milkshakes," I said, overcome with how people in Green showed up for one another.

"Sounds like a bargain to me," Chris said, descending to greet the new arrivals.

After the required baby-admiration ritual, the younger crew picked up paintbrushes and put a fresh white coat on the stucco, the scent of paint mingling with honeysuckle from vines in pine trees behind the building.

Tammy, who had been photographing a city council meeting, snapped the entire process, which included Katy, cute as ever with a splash of white paint on her.

"You look like Holly Beth when she got into that can of green paint last year," Molly said, reaching up to wipe it off with a rag.

Katy laughed and pushed back her hair, this week cut short and dyed jet black, leaving a streak of white paint in it. The hair had given me pause. I had hoped after the Zach job offer that Katy had relaxed some.

"I can't imagine Ellie at that age," Iris whispered.

"Our day is coming," I whispered back.

Dub and Joe patched plaster that had crumbled on the front of the building, and Maria filled a bucket with hot, soapy water and took a toothbrush to the tile tabletops. "This is going to be a very cute place," she said. "It reminds me of where I worked back home in Mexico."

Her voice and good humor charmed me. She was an attractive woman in her thirties and lived in the trailer that had been Chris's before we married.

"Where are your boys tonight?" I asked.

"They're with Pastor Jean." She lowered her voice. "She wants to keep them often. You know, I think that she plans to move closer to her husband."

I nodded. "She thinks of your sons as grandbabies. It'll be hard on you when she leaves."

"Oh, not so," Maria said, and for a moment I thought she'd misunderstood my words. "All things work together for good. No?"

I blinked, absorbing the sounds of happy work around me. "Absolutely," I said.

Within a couple of hours, a subtle shift in the Bayou Freez occurred. It already looked *different.* Old buildings had the strangest way of glowing when they were loved. I'd seen it in the cottage Aunt Helen gave me, and saw it in Chris's grandparents' old home, where we now lived.

"It's all coming together," I said to Chris.

"It's beginning to look like its old self," he said.

Katy scrubbed the oversized freezer, while I worked on the sink. Molly took her turn entertaining Eddie, in his carrier after being passed around for hugs and kisses. Anthony and Luke scraped flaking paint right outside the door.

Chris had gone back to work on the ceiling. With a large tile in his hands, he turned slightly to say something to me. As I looked up, he slipped and grabbed at the ladder. As it tilted precariously toward Eddie, my nimble husband threw himself in the other direction, landing with a resounding thud on the floor.

For maybe two seconds there was silence, everyone trying to figure out what had happened. Then everyone spoke at once, some moving and others frozen.

"Chris!" I shouted. "Are you OK? Somebody help him. Check on Eddie. Is he all right?"

Anthony, who had been seriously injured in a basketball game a year earlier, propped his crutches against the wall and hobbled over to Chris, a worried look on his face. "Coach, can you hear me?"

Molly stood next to Anthony, as though to catch him if he stumbled, and they were joined by Walt and Tammy, who had materialized with the group from outside. The result was a human shield around Chris.

The overall sense of frenzy was accompanied by Katy's dramatics as she leapt over to check the stunned Chris's pulse. "He's not dead," she said proudly. "He just knocked himself out."

At first I thought Chris's eyes had rolled back in his head, but then I realized he was rolling his eyes at Katy's pronouncement. "If everybody will give me a little air," he groaned, "I'll get up off the floor."

He rolled over, moaned as he tried to sit up, grabbed his arm, and stared underneath the bottom shelf of the work area. "This floor is filthy under here," he said, wincing.

"Chris, are you OK?" I pushed through the crowd and knelt beside him.

He frowned and looked intently under the cabinet, while I looked at his right arm, which hung at a weird angle. "There's something under here," he said, straining to retrieve something. "It looks like a box of money."

Then he passed out, Tammy snapping one photograph after another.

The amazing crowd of volunteers unfortunately did not include Kevin or any other medical personnel, but Luke proved to have a calm head and a fair knowledge of first aid.

"I've gone on lots of youth mission trips," he said. "Someone always gets hurt. Let me see."

As he sat on the floor by me, I motioned to Anthony. "Call an ambulance," I said. "We need to get him to the hospital."

"He'll have to go up to Shreveport," Iris said, her hand on my shoulder. "The emergency room's closed."

"I wonder if we can reach Kevin?" I said.

Luke took Chris's pulse again. "Katy, where's your hairbrush?" he asked.

The young woman automatically put her hand to her hair.

"It's in her purse," Molly said, calm in the face of almost anything. "Here."

By now, Chris was rousing. "Is Eddie all right?" he asked.

"Shhh," I said. "He's fine. We'll get you to the hospital. You hit your head when you fell off the ladder."

"What's wrong with my arm?" He tried to sit up. "Luke, why are you holding that hairbrush?"

"We're going to need it for a splint," the young preacher said. "Your bone's sticking through the skin." I wanted to look away from that bone but couldn't.

"Are you sure you know what you're doing?" Chris asked, scrutinizing his arm. His head bobbed as though his neck weren't quite strong enough to hold it up.

"Absolutely," Luke said, looking like nothing was out of the ordinary. "I did this same thing when a buddy broke his arm playing soccer."

Then Katy fainted.

Eddie started crying when the confusion level grew in the kitchen, and I pleaded quietly with God to make everything OK, weakened by the sight of my big, strong husband looking pale. Chris ground his teeth while Luke attached the hairbrush to his crooked arm with duct tape.

"Oooh, Coach," Anthony said, swallowing hard. "Pulling that tape off is going to hurt worse than the broken arm."

Molly knelt down by Katy.

"Thanks for taking care of her," Luke said, glancing over at the two young women. "Her color's good, but she probably needs a wet cloth on her face."

Eddie wailed as if disagreeing with all that was going on, and Tammy took him from me. She walked outside, calming him with a song as she went. I grabbed a dishtowel and dunked it in a jug of ice water on the counter. Katy's eyes fluttered open when I put the cloth on her face. "That bone was disgusting," she said, groaning.

"Good thing you didn't choose a medical profession," Luke said. "You OK?"

"I feel lightheaded," she said. With her head on the old tile floor, she turned toward the wall, her eyes widening. She scooted closer to the edge of the worktable and reached under the counter, wrinkling her nose. "There must be a hundred years of dirt under here. Lois, hand me that broom, please."

I stared at her.

"Lois," she said more urgently. "Get that broom."

"Quit fooling around," I snapped. "Chris is hurt. I'm not worried about the dust."

"It's not dust," she said, sliding her thin body nearly under the table. "Chris was right. There's a box of money under here."

Kevin was striding in the door with her medical bag as Katy pulled out a shoebox, the lid askew and a packet of hundred-dollar bills peeking out.

"Hey, Doc," Chris said, sounding more clearheaded than I felt. "I've busted my arm."

"I fainted," Katy said, standing up so quickly she had to steady herself by holding onto the cabinet. "And we found a pile of money."

Kevin, wearing her lab coat, met my eyes with one of her concerned physician smiles and began to take Chris's blood pressure. "Have you two ever thought of taking up a nice boring hobby?"

Then she examined his arm, shaking her head slightly. "You've got a compound fracture. We need to get you to Shreveport. I hope you're prepared for surgery."

A child, four dogs, two businesses, a flock of chickens, and a catfish pond made dashing off to surgery even more complicated than expected. Tammy insisted on driving Chris to the hospital, while I tied up loose ends. "Walt will meet me at the hospital, and we'll keep an eye on Chris until you can get there," she said.

"I'll take you when you're ready, Lois," Kevin said. "I can check on Chris and drive home later."

"I'll bring Lois and Chris back in the morning," Tammy said. The two sounded like generals planning an invasion. "It makes sense."

I hated to let Chris go. "Are you sure you don't need an ambulance?" I asked as he settled into the backseat of Tammy's mammoth SUV.

His face was ashen but the customary warmth shone in his brown eyes. He shook his head and touched my hair with his good hand. "This is not that big a deal," he said. "Kevin will call ahead, and they'll get me patched up in no time."

Luke offered to check in at our house and tend the dogs, Iris promised to take good care of the box of money and make sure the *News-Item* went to press the next day. Estelle and Hugh came and got Eddie, which delighted them and broke my heart.

"I've never been away from Eddie overnight," I said to Kevin, who had arranged for Pearl and Marcus to keep her son so she could drive to Shreveport with me.

"I don't know what I'd do without my parents," she said. "They're the only ones I trust with Asa."

I thought of my mother and father, who had died years earlier. "I'm blessed to have great in-laws," I said, as we hit the highway and headed north. "But I wish my parents could have known Chris and Eddie."

As we drove off, the old, yellow lights of the Bayou Freez glowed as a dozen or more people painted and cleaned. Laughing and talking, they looked like a Norman Rockwell painting under the shadow of the big oaks, the inky black of the lake bed behind them.

Chris was groggy, and I was loopy, by the time Tammy picked us up at the hospital early the next morning.

"Oh, no," she said, looking at the huge cast. "Eddie's Daddy has turned into a Mummy." She laughed at her own cleverness and started snapping pictures.

"I'm not in the mood for this, Tammy." I smoothed my hair and covered my face with my hands. "Put that camera up, or you're going to need a cast on both arms."

"Chris should be the grouchy one," she said, for once doing what I said. "He's the one with pins in his wrist and a knot on his head."

Kevin had left as soon as Chris's surgery was over, so once more Chris settled in the back of Tammy's car. He picked up the baseball bat that lay on the back floorboard.

"You still protecting yourself with this?" he asked, wincing as he lay back. I wasn't sure if his response was due to pain or the fact that a drug dealer had once attacked me and Tammy, and she'd scared him off with the bat.

Tammy looked in the rearview mirror, pulling out of the parking lot, and grinned. "Walt doesn't like it either, but it works. Right, Lois?"

"That day ranks right up there with the day my husband fell off a ladder, broke his wrist, and got a concussion," I said. "I'd rather not think about it."

"What's the latest on that guy, anyway?" Chris asked, his voice sounding hazy as he adjusted the pillow propping up his arm. "I assume he's still in jail."

"Walt checked just the other day," Tammy said, clearing her throat. "He's about to get out on parole."

"He'd better stay away from North Louisana," Chris said and drifted off to sleep.

"Why didn't you tell me Vince was getting out of jail?" I asked.

"I was going to," Tammy whispered, "but there's always so much going on. I had that doctor's appointment down in Houston and you've had the Freez."

"Any more word from those tests you had?"

"No." She put on her turn signal and changed lanes. "I'll let you know if anything happens."

I pulled down the visor and looked in the mirror, double-checking that Chris was asleep. "Did Walt learn anything else about the parole issue?"

"The word is that Vince is moving to Oklahoma. Walt made it clear to the court that we don't want him anywhere near Bouef Parish. Does Anthony ever mention him?"

"Anthony despises him," I said. "Vince called once from jail, but Anthony's mother refused the charges."

I sagged against the seat. The cool leather felt good against my arms. After pulling through a fast-food restaurant for coffee, we headed south on Interstate 49, the eastern sky lightening and a faint glow of pink shining through a bank of clouds. Traffic headed north was especially steady, despite the early hour, with fleets of white oilfield trucks whizzing past us.

"Who are all these people?" I sipped the steaming coffee.

"People who work in Shreveport, I guess," Tammy said. "The traffic's heavy every day when I come to work."

Sitting here in Tammy's vehicle had taken on the feel of an overnighter at college, where you stay up too late and are ready to tackle the problems of the world. "This interstate's handy," I said, "but it sucks the personality out of little communities." I pointed at the huge neon sign of a truck stop and video-poker casino.

"Do you think there's really any chance for little towns to survive?" Tammy asked.

"Most towns can't make it, but I hold out hope for Green."

"Me, too."

Exiting onto the bypass on the edge of town, we hit a bump, and Chris moaned in his sleep but didn't wake up.

Eddie bounced up and down in his swing attached to the doorframe, while I sorted the stacks of magazines, bills, and junk mail that had accumulated in the past few days.

A postcard from Marti and Gary, my best friend in Dayton and her husband, stuck out from between a catalog and a magazine. "Look, Eddie." I sat on the floor next to where he played and held up the card from Scotland. "Aunt Marti and Uncle Gary say Scotland is beautiful, and they're meeting tons of nice people." He didn't seem too interested, playing with his toe instead.

I pointed to the rocky coastline pictured on the card. "I want you to see all the beautiful places in the world, little guy."

"Planning a trip?" Chris walked in from feeding his catfish, his big cast white against his tan skin. He planted a kiss on both of our foreheads.

I held the card up. "Look where Marti and Gary spent the weekend."

Chris studied it. "I wonder what kind of fish they catch there?"

"They're sightseeing more than fishing," I answered absently, examining the photo, while Chris lifted Eddie from the swing and held him with one arm.

Still sitting on the floor, I sighed.

"Something bothering you?" Chris asked, jiggling Eddie up and down.

"Do you think Green's a good place to live?" I asked.

"Sure," he said. "Especially since you and Eddie came along."

"What about all the other great places out there?"

He frowned and turned his attention away from Eddie to me. "Green's home," he said. "I hope we have money to travel when Eddie's older, but I'm happy right out here on Route Two. Aren't you?"

"Some days I worry that Green can't offer Eddie enough," I said. "I want our son to have the best of everything."

"He'll have a great life here," Chris said, trying to reach for my hand with his broken arm. "We'll do all we can for him. In fact, right now I think his parents should take him for a walk and teach him what frogs sound like. I bet that's something big city kids don't know."

Sliding my feet into my oldest tennis shoes, I followed Chris and Eddie into the yard, the sight of them and the house reminding me of the many reasons I loved living in Green. If I had to choose from all the places in the world, I figured I'd choose Green all over again.

And I thanked God for bringing me here.

13

Marilyn Wright is looking for the owner of two large chows who entered her home. "They chased Pumpkin up on top of the china cabinet and scared that poor thing to death," she said, "and I don't care for them myself." Police said the dogs entered through the cat door. "I don't think I should have to nail the door shut just because someone can't control their animals," Marilyn said.

—*The Green News-Item*

The uproar over the mystery money had not died down, despite my attempts to find out where it came from and to get everyone else to quit talking about it.

All $23,000 of it.

You can fit more money in a shoebox than I ever realized.

"Cold Cash from Ice-Cream Eatery Still Not Claimed," the headline on Linda's follow-up story read, but the report contained little more than how we discovered the money.

Major Wilson tried to claim the box, since he'd owned the building until two weeks earlier. "It was my property," he insisted, showing up at the newspaper.

Walt, the newspaper's attorney, advised us to let the police deal with it. "Legally it will be yours unless it is stolen property. Let the chief handle it."

The only link to a crime came when police tested the bills and found traces of cocaine. Linda said on the police beat that wasn't uncommon. "The chief says almost all old twenties have drug residue," she told us during our weekly staff meeting.

"Now I have to keep Eddie away from cash when he grows up," I said. Iris Jo threw me a small grin.

"Think how great it would be if we could keep all that cash," Katy said. "We need to figure it out."

"Or give it back to its rightful owner," Molly said. "That could be a little old lady's life savings."

"I wonder if it's been there since the Bayou Freez closed?" Katy asked. "I bet it *is* drug money."

"Or stolen," Tammy said.

"Maybe it's hush money," Molly added and then gave a little smile. "I don't even know what hush money is."

Linda was convinced the cash was tied into the rumors we'd heard about Major, but the police department hadn't yielded a clue. "Doug and I have looked through every case we can think of," she said, "and there's not a hint of missing cash."

"Maybe someone was trying to freeze their assets," Tammy said and looked around to make sure we'd all caught her pun.

"We need to be professional about this," I said. My rare stern-publisher's voice got everyone's attention. "This might be a clue to a big news story." I got up and closed the door. "We're investigating Major's past. Even though we've joked about the money, this is potentially a dangerous story."

"That's what Alex says," Katy said and then quickly started doodling on her tablet. "He always thought Major had done more than swindle people in real estate deals."

"Maybe we need to make a list of suspects and examine each one," Linda said. "Perhaps Major is only part of the puzzle." She left the conference room and returned with a tabletop flip chart and set of markers. Hardly had she taken the cap off the pen before ideas started flying.

"We know it must have been there for a while," Linda mused. "The building's been locked up for years, and Major says he hasn't been in there since long before he went to prison."

"That's not right," Katy and Molly said simultaneously.

"We saw Major and Mr. Dub in there before you bought it," Katy continued.

"They were yelling," Molly said.

"Mr. Dub is nice, but he had motive and method," Katy said.

Motive and method? She sounded like a prosecuting attorney.

"Dub helped his brother steal from the paper," Linda said, "and he and Major used to be friends. Maybe he has something on Major."

Katy's eyes grew huge. "What if Molly was right, and it really is hush money?"

"We can't rule out Major," Stan, who rarely spoke in the meetings, said. "He's the one who had easy access."

"That almost seems too obvious," I said, more to myself than them.

"Major's been complaining about being strapped for cash, so why would he leave a box of money lying around?" Iris Jo asked.

"Maybe someone was supposed to pick it up," Stan said. "Or maybe someone dropped it off and didn't get a chance to communicate with Major."

Molly's brow furrowed. "I've got a weird idea."

"You've obviously come to the right place," Tammy said.

"What about one of those meth dealers we keep hearing so much about? Doug says they're all out in the area."

"The only one I know of is that guy Anthony's mother used to date," I said.

"Anthony says he used to throw Major Wilson's name around like they were best friends," Molly said. "He's supposed to be in Oklahoma or somewhere. He just e-mailed Anthony's mother that he was getting out of jail and moving away. It was sort of a threatening message and really upset Anthony."

"I didn't know inmates had e-mail privileges," Tammy said.

"They're supposed to have limited computer access," Linda said, "but I guess if you're a meth dealer, you're not exactly a rule follower."

"So we're sure he's not around here?" I asked.

"It's possible but unlikely," Linda said, putting his name on the chart. "Maybe he came through after he got out of jail, but he'd be a fool to hang around Green."

"Or he could have hidden the money before he was arrested," Stan said.

Something niggled in the back of my mind, and I thought back to the day Chris and I first looked around the Bayou Freez.

"The door wasn't locked," I exclaimed. "One of the first things we did was ask Lee Hicks to install a new lock."

"That's it!" Tammy said, grabbing a marker off the table and writing Lee's name with a star by it. "Lee Roy had access to the building, and he has stolen before. I never did buy that jailhouse conversion act."

"I don't think it's him," Iris said. "He's worked so hard to do right. I don't see how he would have time to be up to no good."

"That's what they said about Jack the Ripper, too," Tammy said.

"Tammy!" I said.

My thoughts were heavy as I considered the names we'd come up with, and Iris voiced my thoughts. "We're awfully quick with accusations," she said. "Just because people have done wrong in the past doesn't mean they're still living that way."

"Most of the people in the Bible did their best work after they messed up," I reminded them.

"But they had to repent," Iris said quietly.

"Linda, look through all the records again," I said. "If anyone can come up with a clue, it'll be you."

Despite sweltering August heat and the upcoming opening of school, enthusiasm over the renovation of the Bayou Freez climbed steadily, with a regular group of volunteers.

Katy zipped in one night, barely closing her car door as she rushed forward with her laptop. "I've come up with a logo," she said. "What do you think about a big swirl of white ice cream with the cone and the words 'Bayou Freez' in red? It's got a retro feel with a modern twist. Hold on, and I'll show you."

She booted up her computer, smiling as an instant message appeared.

I craned my neck to see what it said.

"It's personal." Katy tilted the screen away from me. "Colt's so romantic."

"So, that's still going on?" My hint of disapproval did not escape Katy's notice.

"He's amazing," she said. "This is serious."

"Have you even met him face-to-face?" I asked.

She shook her head and started to speak, but I interrupted. "Then how can you be in love?"

"We've communicated more online than Alex and I did in person," she said. "Like Colt says, we have a special connection."

"What's he like on the phone?" I asked. The notion of Katy having a "special connection" with some guy none of us had ever met made my discomfort grow.

"He travels a lot with the band and doesn't get back to the room till late," she said. "We're both writers, so we've decided to get to know each other through e-mail. It's much more romantic."

"They don't talk," Molly said, strolling up, hammer in hand. "Katy says it's like when people used to write love letters to each other during the war and stuff," she said. "But I'd miss holding hands and hugging." She threw a shy smile over at Anthony. He had propped his crutches against the counter and was sanding our new plywood menu board.

"I don't want to see you get hurt, Katy," I said.

Nearby Luke hesitated, but then went back to sweeping up a mound of sawdust. "Luke worries just like you do," Katy said, "but everyone's going to love Colt. Now tell me what you think about these logo designs."

"Your cast is made out of the same stuff as these walls," I said, slathering another layer of white paint on a Bayou Freez outside wall.

"My stucco arm," Chris said, sticking a ruler up under the plaster to scratch.

"Does it ache?" I asked.

"Just a little," he said. "Watching you takes my mind off of it."

Chris had refused to stop working on the project, despite the clunky apparatus, and rarely complained about how hard it was to do things with one arm. Even with the cast, he was as graceful as I was on a regular day.

"At least the cast doesn't crumble the way this stuff does," I said, poking at a hollow spot with my paintbrush.

"When did you patch that?" he asked.

"I thought you did," I said.

"I guess Stan or Lee did that, but it's not very even." Chris tapped it harder, and a small hole opened up.

"Careful," I urged, looking around to see if any of our steady volunteers had seen. "I don't want to hurt someone's feelings."

"The only person whose feelings will be hurt," he said, pulling a small object out, "is the owner of this watch." He stuck his ruler in the hole and hollowed it out, extracting a diamond engagement ring, a silver bracelet, and an emerald and ruby bracelet.

"When you said this place was a treasure," he said, displaying the jewelry in the palm of his big hand, "I misunderstood what you meant."

The handful of helpers on hand gathered in seconds, their mouths agape at the loot.

"I wonder what other secrets we're going to uncover?" Katy asked.

"This place is a cash cow," Tammy said.

"Get Doug on the phone," I said with a sigh.

Doug and Linda, who I was certain were unofficially dating, arrived together.

"These items certainly must have something to do with the cash you found," the chief said. "But none of this matches any of our cases."

Sealing the building off for the rest of the evening, Doug and one of his few officers inspected it, and asked each of us for detailed statements. I stood nearby when Joe Sepulvado was interviewed, wanting to make sure that he didn't think he was a suspect.

"It's OK, Miss Lois," Joe said. "We need to find answers." He reached out and clasped Maria's hand and quietly talked to Doug.

"Nothing," the police chief said to me and Chris as the thick night air settled around us like a damp towel. "No one has seen anything. The closest thing to a lead is some old car that drives by every now and then. That fits about three-quarters of the residents of Green."

"You're going to need a security guard for a while, Coach," Doug said. "Every Tom, Dick, and Harry will be gouging chunks out of your building otherwise. I'll have one of my guys drive by, but that won't keep people away."

"Maybe Lee Hicks would take that job," Chris said. "He needs extra work so he can get his own place."

The chief frowned. "The department doesn't recommend ex-cons as guards," he said. "And we haven't ruled him out as a suspect. We're still trying to trace that money, and the jewelry is almost certainly stolen."

Chris absently adjusted his sling and shook his head. "Lois and I vouch for Lee," he said. "My father says the good Lord has worked on that man's heart."

"Every reformed criminal says that," Doug said, "but it takes a miracle for these people to stay clean."

"It might be a miracle," I said, "but Lee has changed."

"I don't understand why you think so highly of Lee Roy Hicks," the chief said. "You're the one who turned him in in the first place."

I thought of Eddie's and Holly Beth's affection for Lee and how hard the man had worked to pay the newspaper back. He was tender as he got to know his daughter. "Wherever this leads us," I said, "it won't be to Lee."

Chris murmured his agreement and scratched his arm with the ruler again.

"Evenings here remind me of the old days," Chris said as we took a break on one of the tables under the portico, eight or ten friends scurrying around with clean-up supplies, "except we still don't have any ice cream."

"The new machines should be delivered in a few days," I said. "Ready or not, we're about to be in the milkshake business."

"Have you figured out who's going to run this place?" Tammy asked as she zoomed her lens in on Eddie and Ellie in a playpen swathed with mosquito netting.

"We're open to suggestions," I said. "You want the job?"

"Not as manager," she said, "but I might be interested if you hire a flavor consultant." She took a few more pictures of the group. Then she frowned and extended the telephoto lens, clicking the shutter.

"There's that car again." Tammy's voice came out as a growl. "That guy gives me the creeps."

"What guy?" I asked.

Tammy was exasperated. "That guy I told you about the other day. He keeps driving by. I even mentioned it to Doug the night you found that stuff in the wall."

My quick scan of the street showed the car, an old Chevy Nova like one of my dad's friends had owned, rolling away from the drive-in. "Maybe we should call the police," I said.

Tammy picked up her camera, partially hiding behind a post while the car turned and came back by. "I wonder if he could have something to do with the money?"

A baseball cap obscured the driver's face, and he was slouched over in the seat but clearly looking at the Bayou Freez.

"He's watching Katy," Tammy hissed.

I turned to catch sight of Katy, laughing and talking to Molly as she walked over to where we were. As I looked back, the driver slipped lower into the seat.

"Katy, do you know that guy?" I asked. Tammy pointed the camera at him and took a series of photos.

"Creepy," Katy said, shaking her head. "I don't know him, and I don't want to."

The driver made an obscene gesture and peeled out with an obnoxious roar.

I snapped my fingers. "We've seen him before! He's the nut who broke through the ribbon the day the highway opened!"

The future of the Bayou Freez was shaping up. Even Pastor Jean, still not saying when she expected to leave, got wrapped up in the discussions.

Stopping by our house one Sunday after church, she sank appreciatively into a red Adirondack chair and sighed. "This feels like heaven."

Chris was taking a rare nap with Eddie, and I had been reading. The ceiling fan stirred enough air to keep us from melting. The hum of our conversation reminded me of Sunday afternoons as a child, when I could hear my mother talking quietly in another room.

"I've been praying about the need for jobs in Green," she said, "and I hope you and Chris might feel led to use that drive-in as a ministry of sorts . . . I thought you might provide training for the youth who can't find jobs and maybe a few of the participants in our Spanish ministry."

"Chris suggested that a couple of weeks ago," I said. "We've had so much help getting it ready that we both see that it's a special place."

"You have a way of creating special places," she said, looking around the porch.

"We need a good manager, though," I said, touched by her compliment. "We can't pull that off without someone to organize it. Neither one of us has a spare second."

We looked at each other.

"Joe Sepulvado," I said.

"He needs steady work," Jean said, nodding vigorously. "He's mature and wise. He'd be perfect. He ran a small grocery store in Mexico." She paused. "His English is improving, and he's got a kind heart."

"Perhaps Dub will mentor Joe," I said. "That would give him something to do besides play golf, and Dub's got an interest in the Freez."

"I have another idea, too, as long as I'm spending your money," she said, the fan kicking up small wisps of dark hair around her face. "Consider hiring Maria part-time. She and Joe make a fantastic team at Kids' Club on Wednesdays."

"She works hard at the school," I said. "She keeps that place spotless. But I don't know how we'd pay two employees. I'm not sure how we're going to pay for one."

"We'll pray about it for the next few days," Jean said, putting her tea on a stone coaster and rubbing her hands together. "Something will work out."

I smiled. "I wish I'd known this when I was younger. All things apparently do work together for good."

"Amen, Lois Barker Craig," my pastor said. "Amen."

14

The area's smallest village has more voters than voting-age residents. A voting clerk at the Kickapoo precinct has asked officials to look into whether numbers are right or wrong. "This is crazy," said precinct captain Alan Blair. "People who don't really live here think they can come here and vote when we've never seen hide nor hair of them before."

—The Green News-Item

The glare of the late summer sun blinded me as I accelerated onto the bypass heading to work, already missing Eddie, who had stayed home with Chris.

In hindsight, today would have been a good day to take the old route to work, but I had been spoiled by the convenience of the new road and was irritated when the traffic in front of me came to a halt.

Follow-up workers, who posted "Do Not Litter" signs and planted small magnolia trees, occasionally slowed me down, but this was the first time traffic had stopped altogether.

"Is this really necessary?" I muttered, and Holly Beth, in her crate, whined and gave a sharp bark.

With no traffic across the grassy median, I fidgeted in my seat and realized I'd left my coffee cup on the kitchen counter.

In the next ten minutes, I stuck my neck out the window, trying to see what was happening over a small hill, filed my nails, and tried to call the newspaper. I scrolled through pictures of Eddie on my cell phone, which was better at taking photos than it was at making calls.

Smiling at one of my son's slobbery grins, I nearly dropped the phone when it rang, glancing down to see Tammy's number.

"I'm stuck in traffic on the bypass," I said. "First time I've ever been caught in rush-hour traffic in Green."

"I was calling to tell you to go the other way," she said. "I heard something about a wreck on the police radio, and I'm headed out to see if I can get pictures for tomorrow's paper."

"I'll see if I can find out anything," I said.

"Lois?" Tammy's voice echoed in my ear. "I'm having a hard time hearing you. Iris Jo's at the office. I'll call you later."

Throwing the phone on the seat in disgust, I eased the SUV onto the shoulder and rolled the front windows down, the faint sound of sirens in the distance.

I grabbed a notebook and pen from my purse, opened the door, and turned slightly. "I'll be right back," I told Holly Beth, who I knew would be miffed at me for leaving her.

After I took a few steps on the edge of the road, the driver of the car in front of me got out, shielded her eyes from the sun, and looked up the road in front of us.

"Can you see anything?" I asked, recognizing her from the checkout line at the grocery store.

"Not with this sun in my eyes," she said. "I'm going to be late for work if they don't let us pass soon."

As I walked past the dozen or so cars in front of me, drivers, some of whom I knew from church or civic groups, rolled down their windows and spoke or stood by their cars visiting. The day was already warm, and heat radiated off the pavement.

"It's a bad wreck," one man, closer to the top of the hill, said. "They can't get the driver out of the second car."

"Any idea who it is?" I asked.

"They're not saying."

Walking faster, I topped the hill and could see the flashing lights of two sheriff's department cars, a Green patrol car, a rural EMS vehicle, and a city fire truck. One car, mangled beyond recognition, lay in a ditch to my right, and the other was upside-down in the middle of the highway, a hundred yards or so away.

Emergency personnel swarmed like bees around one of my father-in-law's hives.

Drawing closer, I ran through the names of people I knew, relieved with each person I ruled out. Chris and Eddie were at home, Iris was at the paper, and that meant Stan and Ellie probably were, too. Tammy was on her way to the scene, and Estelle and Hugh had been working in their garden since daylight, so it couldn't be them.

Before I went further, a man walked toward me, and I squinted, trying to see who it was.

"Don't come any closer, Miss Lois." As the figure blocked my way, I recognized Wayne, a Bouef Parish sheriff's deputy. "You don't need to see this."

"Do you know who it is?" I asked, holding up my notebook to vouch that I was on business.

"I'd better not say." Wayne looked pained. "We've got to get these people to the hospital and notify their kin before you start spreading the word."

Over his shoulder, I saw workers extract a person from the car that had turned over and lay him or her on a stretcher. A loud whirring noise rumbled overhead, and a helicopter touched down on the other side of the highway.

A radio, attached to Wayne's shirt, squawked, and he spoke quietly into it before turning back to me. "You stay put," he said and sprinted toward the wreckage, his overweight body moving faster than I would have thought possible.

Despite the heat, my blood ran cold as I watched someone kneel by two bodies, the glare obscuring the details, and I moved closer as they loaded only one of the two into the helicopter.

Tammy appeared on the other side of the road, shooting photographs as the helicopter took off. Doug, the chief of police, walked to her side, said something, and wiped his eyes underneath his sunglasses.

Tammy's arm fell, the camera bouncing from the strap around her neck, and she turned, saw me, and shook her head.

I started in their direction, but Doug held up his hand. "No," he yelled. "Stay where you are, Lois."

I ran toward them.

Tammy put her hands over her face and kept shaking her head. I noticed the debris, including a woman's shoe, a plastic water bottle, and a Bible, its loose pages scattered along the right-of-way.

The police chief and Tammy met me before I got close enough to see more.

"I'm sorry, Lois," Doug said.

"Who?" It was the same question I'd asked when I heard about tornado fatalities.

"Miss Pearl and Mr. Marcus," Tammy said and threw her arms around me, the camera sandwiched between us. "Mr. Marcus is dead, and Miss Pearl is in critical condition. Becca's grandmother was driving the car that hit them."

"The police think Becca's grandmother was blinded by the sun and swerved into the other lane," Linda said late that afternoon in the newsroom. The older woman and Pearl had been airlifted to a Shreveport hospital and remained in critical condition.

"The Taylors were going to see someone from their church," I said. "Kevin said her daddy wanted to pray with the woman before she had surgery next week."

"How's Kevin?" Iris Jo asked, walking in from the office with Ellie on her hip.

"In shock," I said. She's with her mother in Shreveport. Terrence is there, too, of course. Molly's staying with Asa, and I'm going back over there in a few minutes."

"Have you talked to Becca?" Tammy asked.

I nodded. "She's at the hospital, worried, heartsick." I reached for Ellie and hugged her, wanting to go home and gather Eddie close. "Her grandmother is conscious, but they haven't told her about the Taylors."

"I wish she didn't have to know," Iris whispered. "No one should have to bear such a burden."

"How could you live with yourself?" Katy said. "Knowing you killed someone."

"It was an accident," Tammy said.

"She probably shouldn't have been driving," Linda said, "but I know from my parents how hard it is to give up your car."

"Poor little Asa," Tammy said. "First his Papa Levi and now his Papaw."

"Not to mention his birth mother and two siblings," I said. "That child has lost more already than many people do their whole lives."

"Thank goodness Asa has Kevin," Iris said, reaching for Ellie.

"Why don't you go home to Eddie and Chris?" Tammy asked. "The next few days are going to be tough."

I hesitated. "There's something I need to do first." Tears welled in my eyes and dripped onto my cheeks as I dug around in a desk drawer.

Walking through the lobby to the front of the building, I thought of my first meal with a family in Green. It was a home-cooked supper with the Taylors, a meal that welcomed me to Green and gave me a glimpse into what my life would become.

My staff surrounded me as I painted the name of Marcus Taylor on the *Item* window, next to the names of others who had died since the paper's last edition. "Good and faithful servant," I wrote under his name and bowed my head.

"Welcome Marcus home, O, God," I said.

A chorus of "amens" echoed through the lobby, and baby Ellie clapped her hands.

The loss of one of Green's most caring civic leaders and the horror of his death threatened to sap any spirit of renewal right out of Green.

Becca temporarily closed her store to tend to Cassie and help with her brother. Her mother and Kevin spent most of their time at the hospital in Shreveport.

The darkened flower shop, with a faded wreath on the door, symbolized how most of us felt.

Kevin moved through the ordeal with the grace she always exhibited, but her rich brown eyes were dull with grief. She was exhausted from her bedside vigil, mixed with the pain of planning her father's service. Her mother remained in critical condition and couldn't attend the memorial service, making a heartbreaking day even harder.

"It doesn't seem real," Kevin said repeatedly after the service. The tribute had included an array of photographs and memorabilia from her father's life and nearly two hours of testimonials from friends and family, laughter and tears brought together with fierce hugs.

Today, three days later, Asa was riding a shiny red bike with training wheels when I arrived. Terrence's hand rested on his back. "Look, Miss Lois, I'm riding," Asa called out. "Daddy Terrence gave me a bike."

The big man smiled at the boy and looked back at me with a face filled with sorrow. "All I can do for Kevin is be here for Asa." He spoke quietly after encouraging Asa to ride a little way down the sidewalk.

"I talked Kevin into staying home this afternoon. She's lying down." He glanced around to make sure Asa was out of earshot. "It's sinking in that her father isn't coming back."

"I don't want to disturb her if she's sleeping," I said. "Maybe I should come back later."

"She's not asleep," he said, wiping his eye. "She needs you."

Letting myself into the bungalow Kevin had bought and renovated, I drank in the coziness of the home. The signs of normal, everyday life—Asa's favorite plastic dump truck and an assortment of books—intersected with a hodgepodge of sympathy cards on the coffee table and baskets of wilting plants.

An array of casserole dishes and bowls were stacked on the bar, and I wondered if I should return them to their owners.

"Kevin," I called out lightly, walking back to her bedroom, usually bright and cheerful but today with the blinds closed and no lights on. "You up for company?"

When she nodded, I sat on the edge of her bed and touched her arm. Her hair, always elegantly styled in a French twist, was pulled back in a stubby ponytail, and her eyes were swollen.

Each time I had seen Kevin since the accident, I had agonized over what to say. Today I said nothing, my own heart breaking at the pain on her face.

"I can't believe this is real," she said. "Daddy's gone, isn't he? And Mama's barely hanging on." She acted as though she would get up. "I need to get back to the hospital. I shouldn't have stayed home."

Instead of speaking, I opened my arms and held her when she started sobbing. I rubbed her back the way I'd seen her rub Asa's dozens of times. My shoulder was damp by the time she lifted her head and reached for a tissue on the bedside table.

"I didn't mean to let loose like that," she said, touching the wet spot on my blouse. "I didn't cry that hard when they came to my office to tell me."

"It's OK," I said. "Cry all you want."

"How are you doing?" she asked, sitting up straighter and staring into my tear-filled eyes.

"I loved him so much," I said. "I know God sent your parents to me when I moved to Green."

Kevin offered a tiny smile. "From the day they heard that you owned the *Item,* they were determined you and I should be friends. 'She must be a strong woman like you,' they told me."

"Your Dad was so proud of you and Asa," I said.

She took a deep breath and nodded.

"Do you remember that first supper?" I asked.

"Mama pulled out all the stops," Kevin said. "She didn't make biscuits and gravy for every visitor."

"And that blessing your father gave! That was the first time I'd been shaken to the core by a prayer. He prayed for me and for you." I smiled tearfully at the memory. "His voice was so deep, and he spoke with conviction."

"Daddy had convictions, all right," Kevin said. "So did Mama. After supper they sat you down in the living room, pulled out their talking points, and started preaching."

"They made Green a better place," I said. "They wanted it to be better for our children."

"They were activists before we knew what that word meant," she said. "They did everything with love, even when people spit on them in the sixties."

"The entire town is mourning with you," I said. "Eva has the flags at half-mast, and people have made a shrine of flowers and gifts over at the motel."

"Have you heard anything . . ." Kevin faltered and started again. "Have you heard anything about that woman who hit them?"

I nodded. "They told her yesterday that your father was killed in the wreck and that your mother is in ICU. She tried to get out of the hospital bed to come see you."

"They should have taken her driver's license away," Kevin said. "She couldn't see well enough to drive."

I collected my thoughts before I responded. "She passed her last exam. Becca has gone over it again and again and can't figure it out."

Kevin drew a deep breath. "I wonder if Daddy might have lived if the hospital emergency room had still been open. Or, if Mama could have been treated sooner?"

Their crumpled car flashed before my eyes, a sight I was thankful Kevin had not seen. I slowly shook my head. "Doug said your father never suffered. It happened quickly, Kevin."

"How am I going to live without him? And what if Mama passes?" Kevin asked. "How am I going to get through this?"

"I don't know," I said honestly. "We can only take this a day at a time. I'm here for you. And I know God is with us."

Summoning the nerve to face Becca and her grandmother was harder than holding Kevin while she wept.

"Maybe you should go," I said to Chris at breakfast one morning. "You're a lot better in these situations than I am." I tore the crust off a piece of cinnamon toast and twirled it in my hand, watching our son exhibit his sitting-up skills on a pallet near the living room door.

My husband, wrapping up the last weeks of his summer vacation with babysitting and fix-up chores, rubbed my arm. "If you want me to go, you know I will," he said. "But you're closer to Becca and know her family better. I figure she needs you."

"I hope Becca understands how crazy things have been around here," I said, "and doesn't think I've been avoiding her."

"Have you?" Chris asked, slipping Holly Beth a sliver of bacon.

"Yes," I confessed. "I don't know what to say or do. Her grandmother killed one of the best people on the face of the earth. What am I supposed to say to make that better?"

"You'll say the right thing," he said. "She probably needs someone to listen as much as anything. You're a great listener."

"I'm not," I said. "You're the great listener. I butt in and boss people around."

"True," he said, "but you also help people figure things out about themselves."

I put the uneaten bread on my plate, and Chris abruptly pulled me into an embrace. "You give this old house its heart and keep me and Eddie on track. I love you."

"I love you so much," I said and voiced the thought that had been in my mind since the day of the wreck. "What if that had been you and Eddie on the bypass that day?"

"Shh." Chris put his fingers on my mouth. "We can't understand a tragedy like this. Maybe some day we will, but until then we have to do the best we can."

Those words and the sense of calm that had settled upon me helped as I stepped into the hospital elevator in Shreveport and pushed the button for the ICU floor.

The last time I'd been in that waiting room was when Anthony had been hurt, and the antiseptic smell was the same when I stepped off the elevator.

On those visits, the waiting room was often filled with rambunctious high-school students and an assortment of teachers and Green residents. This afternoon, though, the room was quiet except for a pair of visitors crying near the coffee pot.

Becca sat alone and to the side, her eyes swollen, her back stiff and her chin set. She stared at a painting of women in old-fashioned dresses picking berries. Her grief mirrored Kevin's so closely that I was taken aback. "Becca?" I said softly. "How's your grandmother?"

"Oh, Lois." She shook her head slightly as though bringing herself back from another place. "You didn't have to come all the way up here."

She started to get up, but I sat down next to her, in an uncomfortable straight-backed chair. I wondered why she hadn't chosen one of the many comfortable overstuffed chairs. "Everyone in Green is thinking about you and your family," I said.

"I'm sure they are." She covered her face with her hands. "I'm so sorry, so very very sorry. All of us are." Her words were muffled by her hands.

Uncomfortable in a way I'd never been, I begged God to tell me what to say. An image of Chris at the breakfast table popped into my mind, his encouraging words, his shaggy brown hair and kind eyes, Eddie playing just beyond.

"It was an accident," I said, putting my hand on Becca's shoulder. "Everyone knows that."

She lowered her hands but sat in the frozen position, little resemblance to the lithe, cheerful woman I'd seen only days before. "I shouldn't have let her get her license renewed, but she was seeing fine after her cataract surgery."

"It wasn't your fault," I said.

"In a way it was," she said. "I was supposed to go to the grocery store for her the day before, but I got so busy I never made it. She needed milk."

Despite my resolve not to break down in front of her, tears formed in my eyes. "I should have stopped by more often," I said. "Chris or I could have easily picked up groceries for her."

Becca waved off that sentiment. "How's Miss Pearl? And Kevin? Are they . . . OK?"

"They're getting there," I said. "Kevin's trying to get back to work but still see her mother. She hasn't quite figured out the details yet."

"Who's taking care of her son?" Becca asked the question young mothers seemed to think of first.

"People are lining up to keep Asa," I said with a smile, wanting to ease the mood in any way I could. "Molly and Maria are helping for a couple of weeks. He goes to preschool at the Baptist church a couple of days."

"He's just a little older than Cassie," she said. "I feel so bad that his grandpa is gone, and his grandmother . . ."

I wrapped my arms around her as I had done Kevin. "Becca, you need to forgive yourself."

"How can I?" she asked.

I thought of Pastor Jean and the times I'd gone to her with similar questions, of the pain of my mother's death; Tom, who had died trying to warn us that a tornado was coming during our wedding; and Joe Sepulvado, who had been unjustly accused of arson. I recalled Aunt Helen, who had taken me under her wing when I moved to Green and died when I still needed her so.

"It won't be easy," I said. "I wish I could tell you differently. But you can because of grace . . . and mercy. So many people care about you and your grandmother."

"How will Grandma live with what she's done?" Becca asked. "How do we live with it?"

I reached for Becca's ice-cold hands, clutched in her lap.

"I only know of one way," I said. "We do it together."

15

The Stonewall Ladies Exercise Class is celebrating its fifth anniversary at the Recreation Center after class on Tuesday with a potluck lunch. Members, who are proud to say they're "mostly in their eighties," sit in chairs to exercise. Arlea Mae Kimball has been part of the group the full five years and says, "We don't really work off all the calories we take in, what with all the pastries we share, but I sure do look forward to the class."

—*The Green News-Item*

There it is again," Molly said.

Luke looked up. "Why is that guy hanging around here so much?" he asked.

"I don't like it." Katy frowned.

The redone car that Tammy had pointed out sat down the street from the Bayou Freez on a hot Saturday evening. Tonight the driver got out and leaned against the other side of the car, looking at the lake.

"Given all that's happened around here, we probably need to notify the police," I said, looking around for Chris. He touched up paint with his one good arm.

"What's going on?" Tammy said, walking up from behind me with Walt. "Do I need to call Doug?"

"I don't know," I said. "I don't want to blow this out of proportion, but that guy makes me nervous."

"What's he done?" Walt said, inching closer to Tammy.

"Nothing so far," I said. "He sits in the car and watches us."

"He loiters," Katy said.

"Has he approached anyone?" Walt asked.

"Not yet," I said. "This is the first time we've noticed him out of the car."

"He doesn't seem aggressive," Walt said, studying the man. "I wonder if he lives around here?"

"I don't think so," Tammy said. "He hangs around. That expression on his face is like he's mad about something."

"He hasn't really done anything," I said, still uneasy. "But . . ."

"I'll talk to Chris about it," Walt said. "Hold off on the police, but let's keep an eye on him for now."

As he walked off, I gave Tammy a quick hug. "What are you doing here, anyway? I thought you and Walt had plans. You said you weren't going to make it."

"I don't want to give you the big head or anything, but Walt and I admire what you're doing," she said. "We want to be part of this."

"You don't even live here," Katy said.

"I work here," Tammy said. "Now, where do you need me?"

"I'm not sure," I said, unwilling to take my eyes off the stranger.

"Leave him to Walt and Chris," Tammy said. "They won't let anything happen to us."

"Luke, will you keep an eye out over here? If anyone sees anything out of the ordinary, let me know," I said.

With the words just out of my mouth, the man got in the car and drove off.

"Whew!" Katy said. "I'm glad to see him gone."

"Me, too," I said. "Now, let's think about where I can put Tammy to work."

"I want the window," Tammy said. "You promised I could practice again."

"You just like talking people into trying different flavors," I said.

"The chocolate mint is delicious," Tammy said. "But the wedding cake is my favorite. Put hot fudge on it, and it's fantastic."

Getting ready to open the Bayou Freez felt like playing a giant game of Monopoly, with people coming and going behind the counter, arguing over who made the best cones dipped in chocolate and who could fill a shake to the brim without it oozing over the side.

The tip jar that sat on the counter went to missions at church and overflowed with dollar bills most nights, even though nonpaying volunteers were our only customers so far.

"I'll be inside in a couple of minutes," I said.

I walked over to Maria, who was washing windows. As I moved, I looked around, feeling like one of our hens checking on her chicks.

"The restaurant looks lovely," Maria said. "It's a beautiful place. My parents had a café in Mexico. A very happy place."

"That's what we want this to be," I said. "Very, very happy."

Out of the corner of my eye, I saw the suspicious car cruise back into its regular spot. The driver parked and emerged, starting across the street. Tammy turned to pick up her camera bag, and she paused, tilted her head, and gave a small frown before heading into the kitchen.

Chris and Walt each watched from their work areas. I sat down on a bench, missing Eddie, who was with Estelle and Hugh, but glad he was safe. Katy and Molly had ambled to the window, acquiescing to Tammy's suggestion of fresh peach ice cream but keeping an eye over their shoulders.

While they chattered, the driver of the much-discussed car sauntered closer.

"It's an old dude, and he's coming over here," Katy whispered in a nervous voice. She stepped closer to Luke.

"He's not all that old," I said. A baseball cap shielded the man's face, and he wore a loose-fitting Hawaiian print shirt and a baggy pair of jeans. "He's probably not much over thirty."

"We're not open for business," Chris said, coming around the corner of the Freez, his stance assertive. He threw a look at Walt, who gave the slightest shrug. "If you'll stick a donation in that jar there, we'll take a stab at serving you, though."

The man frowned and adjusted his cap lower, but walked on toward the window.

When Tammy leaned out to take his order, he muttered something I could not hear and looked away.

"Are you sure you want vanilla?" Tammy's voice carried across the patio, and I moaned softly. "How about banana pudding? It's our newest flavor."

"I said I want vanilla," the man said, his volume turned up a notch. "If I wanted banana pudding, I'd have ordered banana pudding." He looked at his fancy gold watch, which didn't quite match the rest of him. "I don't have all night."

Chris, his arm still wrapped but not in the sling, and Walt each moved closer, but remained a few feet away. Tammy, separated from him by the window, wore her classic Tammy-about-to-go-off look. I stood and hurried over.

"Is there a problem?" I asked.

Instead of answering, Tammy peered more intently at the customer, her eyes widening. "You're that jerk who attacked me and Lois," she said, her voice not cowed as some women's might have been.

I, on the other hand, took a step back and looked more closely. Standing not a foot away from me was Vince, Anthony's mother's former boyfriend, the abusive meth dealer.

"I thought you were in Oklahoma," I said, just as Anthony hobbled up on his crutches.

"What're you doing here?" Anthony demanded. He looked strong and threatening, despite his injury.

"Anthony," Luke said in a calm, warning way from behind me, as Chris moved closer. Molly and Katy stood a few feet away, a look of shock in their eyes.

"Well, if it isn't Anita's boy, all grown up," Vince said with a sneer. "How is that sweet mama of yours since she got me thrown in jail?"

Anthony lunged forward, dropping one of his crutches, but Luke grabbed his arm. "Don't do this," the preacher said so softly I could barely hear him. "We'll take care of this."

"He beat my mother," Anthony said, staring at the drug dealer, a hint of a hurt child reflected on his angry face. "I should have done something about it a long time ago."

"Anthony," I said, "he can't hurt her anymore. He's out of your life."

"Let's get out of here," Molly said, tugging on Anthony's T-shirt.

"Yeah, this creep isn't worth the effort," Katy said.

Vince sneered and focused on Katy. "Well, that's not what you usually say," he said in a voice that was so sinister my skin crawled.

"Like I'd talk to *you*," Katy snapped. "Get real."

"Did you enjoy the movie in Shreveport last weekend?" Vince asked.

"How'd you know I went to the movie?" she asked, her eyes wide.

"Are you stalking her?" Luke demanded, stepping closer.

"Now, why would I stalk her when she's crazy about me?"

"The only one who's crazy around here is you," Anthony said.

"That's not true, is it, my little Katy-Belle?" Vince said.

Katy's eyes opened even wider, and she stepped back so quickly I thought she was going to fall.

"You're prettier in person than you are in your pictures," the man said. "But you didn't tell me your new preacher friend was so young and good-looking. I guess you haven't told him about us."

An uneasy hush had fallen over the group, and I saw Walt restrain Tammy, who was trying to come outside.

"You need to move on, buddy," Chris said, face-to-face for the first time with the man who had threatened Tammy and me when we'd delivered food to Anthony's family. "If you know what's good for you, you'll go back to Oklahoma and not show your face here again."

My husband's tone was so fierce and unlike him that I considered taking a step back.

"I haven't done anything wrong," Vince said, "and I'm not leaving until I get a vanilla milkshake." He turned to Tammy in the window. "I said vanilla. Not banana pudding."

Tammy squinted.

Chris stood at attention.

I'd never seen him in a fight, but I could tell he was considering punching Vince. Anthony seemed to have similar thoughts, and even Luke was apparently reconsidering his "turn the other cheek" philosophy.

Molly was practically glued to Anthony's back, and Katy's face had a gray tint that reminded me of Chris's when he broke his arm.

"Who are you?" Katy said in an anguished whisper.

"Oh, sweet Katy-Belle," he said. "Don't act like you don't know who I am." He ran his eyes up and down her body. "Is that the new outfit you bought with your friend Molly the other day?" He shifted to a seductive purr. "I was looking forward to seeing it when you came to visit."

"Colt?" Katy said, as though she'd taken a blow to the head. "No, it can't be."

Molly turned in alarm, and more words wobbled out of Katy's mouth. "Colt's in college and sweet and funny. Who are you?"

"Stupid girl." Vince propped his elbow on the serving-window ledge. "Do you know how many inmates say they're in college and good-looking and funny? I'm your boyfriend. I just switched a few photos around."

Tammy threw a filled-to-the-brim shake right in his face.

"I'm an idiot," Katy moaned repeatedly as the police chief took statements from those who'd been involved in what turned into a full-blown fight. "Molly tried to tell me, but I wouldn't listen."

Still shaken by Anthony punching Vince and Chris pinning the man to the ground, I found myself once more not knowing what to say. While that approach had soothed Kevin and Becca, it set Katy off on a new round of self-recrimination.

"Stupid, stupid, stupid," she said.

Doug had answered the police call himself and radioed for a squad car to haul Vince down to the station. "With his record, that's enough for now," the chief said. "But we don't have any charges that will stick yet, and you know it."

Walt went into attorney mode. "Did he give you any idea why he happened to show up here? It can't have been a coincidence."

"All he would say was that he met Katy online, and she got what she deserved. He muttered something about Lois, but then he shut up and asked for a lawyer," the chief said.

"He's not new at being arrested," Walt said. "That's clear."

"His record's long," Doug said. "That'll help us hold onto him until we sort this out. But the judge may let him out." He frowned at me. "You should have called me before this got out of hand."

"It happened fast," I said, reconstructing the evening in my mind. "We were going to call you, but then he left." I remembered Vince's stunned look as the ice cream hit his face right before Anthony's fist connected. "We didn't know who he was at first."

"He's been driving by all summer," Tammy said. "I took pictures of his car the first week Lois and Chris bought the Freez."

Doug looked interested. "E-mail me those as soon as you can."

"Did you see that watch he was wearing?" Tammy demanded. "How does someone in jail get a watch like that?"

My eyes met Tammy's. "The jewelry," she said. "He has something to do with that stuff Chris found."

"And the money," I added. "You have to admit, Doug, there must be a connection." I lowered my voice so Katy couldn't hear me. "Vince was a meth dealer, and the police said it might be drug money."

"He's obviously familiar with the area," Tammy interjected.

"I've gone through that list in my mind, too," Doug said, "but we can't keep him without proof."

I met Chris's eyes. "Vince is working for Major," I said. "I'm sure of it."

"Lois, Tammy, we'll follow up on this," Doug said.

"Can't you charge him for being an online predator?" Molly asked, coming over from where Katy sat with her head on a table. "That jerk has a criminal history, and he tricked Katy."

"She's not a minor," Linda said. She'd arrived with Doug. "He lied, sure, but people lie all the time."

"Especially on the Internet," Doug said. "You girls should be more careful."

"Lois and Molly warned me," Katy said, raising her head. "Colt seemed so nice." Her voice trailed off. "But it was all made up. Colt doesn't even exist. I'm an idiot."

"You're not an idiot," Molly said kindly. "You were deceived."

"How did you get involved with him, anyway?" Doug said, holding up his notebook. "I might as well take your statement."

"He saw my *News-Item* blog," she said, "and then he started e-mailing me."

"You never told me that," I said in dismay.

She shrugged. "Lots of students e-mail me," she said, "and they post comments." Her expression shifted. "Or they say they're students. Who knows now? Maybe it's all a big joke."

My mind churned. We had procedures in place to monitor online comments, but we had no way of knowing that people were who they claimed to be—not really.

"Oh, Katy." I stood beside her. "I never meant to put you in danger."

"You didn't put me in danger," she said. "I was the one who started a relationship with him."

"You made a mistake," Luke said, handing her a cup of water. "It could have happened to anyone. Why don't you let me take you home?"

"Is it OK if I leave?" she asked Doug.

The chief nodded, his lips pursed. "Let me know if you hear from that character again."

"Yes, sir," Katy said, looking about twelve, her lip trembling.

"I'd like to see copies of his e-mails if you've still got them," he said, putting the notebook back into his uniform pocket.

Katy blushed. "I kept them all."

"Mama wanted to keep Eddie overnight," Chris said after calling to let them know we were running late. "I told her you'd like to have him with us."

"And you wouldn't?" I tried to smile, but I felt achy after the adrenaline of the fight.

"Absolutely," he said. "I want you both safe and sound in our house. That was a little more excitement than I care for."

I settled into the passenger seat of the SUV, still keyed up. "It's hard not to obsess on how weird people can be. Did you see that look on Katy's face when she realized Vince was her supposed boyfriend?"

Chris shook his head. "I was too focused on getting between you and him. Do you have to be on the front line every time trouble breaks out?"

"I don't plan to be in the middle of things," I said.

He sighed. "I really didn't think even you could make the ice-cream business dangerous."

16

Roberta Morris sends a special thanks to whoever weeded her flowerbed while she was in Coushatta last week. "I had prayed for help with my yard, and when I got home from the doctor, all of my beds were cleaned up," Bertie says. "When I find out who it was, I'm going to make them one of my icebox pies."

—The Green News-Item

Molly talked Katy into playing a computer game, helped her water every plant in the building, and filched a candy bar from Tammy after the paper came out.

"You've got to get over it," I heard Molly say as I tried to finish a column for next Tuesday's edition. I monitored their every move these days.

"Everything's so messed up," Katy said, and the two drifted out of earshot.

Getting up from my desk, I went to the newsroom. "You two OK?" I asked.

"Do you have something you want us to do?" Katy asked. "I can start on next week's calendar."

"I have plenty for you to do, but not today," I said. "Why don't you two head on out? Do something fun."

"I'm not in the mood," Katy said, and Molly sent a quick glance my way.

"You could drive up to Shreveport," I said.

"I suggested that," Molly said, "but Katy nixed that idea."

Katy's short hair, growing out to its usual reddish-blonde color, was stuck back with a clip. She wore an old pair of jeans and an over-sized blue T-shirt. Her demeanor matched her clothes. Molly looked marginally happier, but she, too, carried a layer of worry.

Sitting down on the old settee, I stretched and tried not to think of the work I needed to do. "Maybe we should go for a walk," I said.

"That's a good idea," Molly said. "It'd be good for us."

"That's the best you've got?" Katy asked, but her words lacked their old spunk. "It's way too hot for a walk."

"Come on, Katy," Molly wheedled and looked at me. "We'll check on the Bayou Freez on the way. That way Lois won't feel guilty for leaving early."

"I don't feel guilty," I said.

"You always feel guilty," Tammy said, striding in from the lobby.

"Do you listen to all of my conversations, or is your timing that perfect?" I snapped.

Katy acted as if she might be about to grin, but quickly returned to her stoic stare.

"Lois has the classic superwoman syndrome," Tammy said. "She has to prove that she's the perfect mom, perfect boss . . ."

"Don't forget 'perfect wife and perfect friend,'" I said.

"You don't have to prove anything to us," Tammy said. "We know you're perfect."

"Yeah, right," Katy said. "I'm the one who messes up."

"Katy," Molly rebuked her friend with the one word.

"Katy, you've got to get over this," Tammy said. "It's almost time for you to go back to school, and you're moping around. We all mess up. Look at me. I dropped out of high school, got arrested for shoplifting, and things still worked out."

Standing, I pointed toward the door. "Out. Us. Let's go for a walk." Grumbling, Katy trailed behind Molly, Tammy mouthing the words "good luck" to me as she returned to the reception desk.

The streets of downtown looked anemic when we headed for the park. "Where is everybody?" Katy asked, looking up and down Main Street.

"Wherever they are, they're not shopping downtown," Molly said.

We meandered toward the park, baskets of geraniums hanging from hooks on the old-fashioned light posts.

"What's wrong with people?" I wondered aloud. "Becca's flowers and the benches and crape myrtles look great. Why can't we get more people down here?"

"Hanging baskets aren't enough," Katy said.

"I worked hard to get money donated for those flowers, and I think they're pretty," I said.

"I didn't say they weren't pretty," Katy said. "But people like to go where there are other people. It's so dead no one will come."

"If it's dead because people won't come, and people won't come because it's dead . . ." I let my voice trail. "We're stuck."

"Well, at least parking isn't a problem," Katy said. The quip was the first I'd heard her make since the Vinceident, as Tammy referred to it. "Joking. I'm joking. You know I want things to work out for Green."

"Oh, sure," I said, trying to adopt a playful tone. "You left us as soon as you could. New York. College." I looked up and down Main Street. "I guess Green doesn't have a lot to offer young people."

"I can't believe you said that," Katy said.

"I look at things differently since Eddie was born," I said.

"This is a good town," Katy stopped walking and shuffled from foot to foot. "I wish I didn't have to go back to college."

Molly's mouth flew open. "You're kidding, right?"

"Tell us you're kidding," I said.

"I'm serious," she said. "I could get my degree at LSU in Shreveport."

"Katy," I said, "you love Georgia. You're halfway finished."

"It's a great school," she said, "but I miss y'all."

"Wait a minute," Molly said. "This is about what happened with Vince. You're afraid to go back."

Katy lifted her chin, almost visibly shifting into defensive mode.

"That's not the only reason," she said. "Anyway, why is it such a big deal? You stayed in Green."

"But I'm not staying here forever," Molly protested.

"You're not?" Katy said.

"I've been going to tell y'all," Molly said, looking like she had a bad toothache. "Mama got a promotion, and the nursing home's moving her to Bossier City. I'm moving, too."

My stomach had the same sort of feeling it had when I came over the top of a big Ferris wheel.

"And you didn't even tell me?" Katy asked.

"I was going to tell you a few days ago, but everything's been crazy," she said. "My mom needs me, and it might be interesting to live somewhere else."

"Will you go to school up there?" I asked.

"Of course," Molly said. "Plus, I hope you'll help me get a job at the newspaper."

Katy perked up. "Since Molly's leaving, may I stay here?"

"Absolutely not," I said. "As much as I'd like to have you." I gestured at the vacant street. "I love this town," I said, "but things are changing. You have to go back to school and learn ways to help us in the future."

"Whatever," Katy said. "I did like New York a lot. But I may come back to live in Green one day."

"Me, too," Molly said, draping her arm around her friend's shoulders.

"I'm counting on it," I said. "I plan on you two running the *News-Item* one of these days."

Molly peeled off for the newsroom when we returned to the paper, but Katy followed me into my office.

"May I close the door?" she asked, as it swung shut. Instead of sliding into her regular spot at the front of my desk, she slumped against the door, her hands over her face.

"Katy!" I exclaimed. "Are you all right?"

She held up a hand before I could continue. "I need a big favor."

"Anything," I said. "You know that."

"Even if Chris doesn't like it?" she asked.

"That's a hard question," I said. "I won't deceive him, if that's what you're asking."

"No, no," she shook her head and moved around to a chair, propping her feet on my desk. "I'm not asking you to lie. I want you to talk Doug into letting me visit Vince in jail."

"What?" I yelled the word and started shaking my head. "No way! You're not getting anywhere near that man. He's evil. No."

"I have to, Lois," she said in a voice that seemed even smaller after my rant. "I don't want to go back to school with this hanging over me."

"Nothing's hanging over you," I said. "They're investigating him, and you may not even have to testify."

"That's not what I mean," she said. "I'm tired of feeling like a victim. I need to look him in the eye and . . . well, see that he's just a dumb criminal with bad teeth." She gave a small smile. "In my mind, he's larger than life, and I want to replace that with the way he really looks."

I exhaled and paced around the office, resting against the closed door as she had done. "You're right. Chris is *not* going to be happy about this. Doug might not agree. I'm sure there are all sorts of rules about visiting inmates. And I'll need to check with Walt about the implications."

Katy's head moved up and down slowly, and she stood. "I understand," she said. "But I have to do this."

No one but Vince agreed with the idea, but I wound up at the jail nonetheless. Katy was not to be deterred. I liked that about her.

A deputy admitted Katy and me into the jail visitation area, escorted by Walt, who had insisted he be present. Chris relaxed only marginally when he heard Walt would be with us and that Plexiglas would separate us from Vince.

I held my breath while we waited for him to come from his cell. He wore a standard bright orange prison jumpsuit, but carried himself with the swagger of a thug.

"Well, well, well," he said, his voice muffled through the vent. "I thought the deputy must be smoking crack when he told me you wanted to see me."

Katy had insisted on sitting in the middle chair, right in front of Vince. She sat up straighter as he spoke and glared at him. "Is it true you helped Major Wilson sell drugs?" she asked.

Walt made a choking sound, and I held in a gasp.

Vince let out a string of curses, drawing a reprimand from the guard. "You are one tough kid. I'll give you that," he said after a moment.

"I'm not a kid," Katy said. "Answer me. Is it true you helped run a meth lab for Major Wilson and used the Internet to locate customers?"

"Katy," Walt said in a warning tone, but I shook my head slightly.

"Let her do this," I said behind Katy's back.

"You know I have proof," Katy said. "Remember those hints *Colt* dropped in his e-mails? I might have been stupid enough to fall for your act, but I'm not too stupid to figure out your trail. I'm a reporter. And a good one."

"Guard," Vince said. "These people are bothering me." He stood to leave.

"You don't know what the word *bother* means yet," Katy said, putting her mouth close to the vent and speaking loudly. "I will not stop until you are put away for years. You've terrorized your last innocent target."

Vince turned at her words, and his walk seemed a little less cocky as he disappeared from our sight.

"Let's get out of here," Katy said, but her voice was strong and her steps certain.

Linda slammed down the phone in the newsroom the following Tuesday morning, waving her notebook. "Make room on page one," she said. "I've got a great story."

Stan had come from the production area to see if we were ready to go to press, and he frowned. "This better be good," he said. "We're running late as it is."

Linda didn't seem to listen. She had stood up and marched over to Katy's desk. "Doug sends his regards," she said. A woman who was not prone to smiling, she had a huge grin on her face. "Vince just accepted a plea agreement that will keep him behind bars for years. He's squealing on Major. He confessed to hiding stolen jewelry at several places around town, including in the wall at the Bayou Freez."

"Yes!" Katy said, pumping her fist in the air.

"Let me notify the carriers that we're going to be late today," Stan said.

Standing in the composing room area, I watched them with pride. In some ways, the feeling resembled the feelings I had when I looked at Eddie. They were part of my family.

Major issued a sweeping denial of Vince's claims. "Consider the source," he said when Linda called him, refusing to answer questions. "It's amazing the lies people will tell to save their own hide."

Hardly had Linda finished talking to Major when he called me.

"I'll sue you for everything you've got, even that rundown dairy bar you're so proud of," he yelled. "I will not have my good name dragged through the mud again by your ratty rag of a newspaper."

"I'll tell my attorney to expect your call," I said. And hung up the phone.

17

Michelle Ransburg will repeat her popular class, "The 5 Ws and 1H," at the downtown library from six to seven p.m. Participants will learn to write press releases for their activities and keep accurate club minutes. "If you remember to include the who, what, when, where, why, and how, you can get good publicity," Michelle said.

—The Green News-Item

Kevin, Terrence and Asa Corinthian arrived at the Bayou Freez on bicycles, Asa squealing in delight from his seat on Terrence's bike. Kevin looked fit and not quite as solemn as she had been lately.

"How's your mother?" I hugged her as I asked.

"She's being moved to a rehab unit next week," Kevin said. "She's not strong enough to get around, but she's a remarkable woman. She's doing all she can to get well."

"And you? How's my friend?"

"I'm better," she said.

Asa interrupted the moment, full of questions now that he was five. "Do you really have ten kinds of ice cream?"

"They have all kinds of milkshakes," Molly, who adored Asa, said. She rushed over to help him off the bike. "Want to see?"

"Everything's free," Katy said. I was happy to see the two college girls more lighthearted than they'd been the week before. Walking hand in hand between the two, Asa talked nonstop, the words "bike" and "Terrence" floating back to us.

Terrence and Chris, carrying Eddie, followed. In no time, Eddie would be walking and talking. It seemed impossible.

"Life goes fast, doesn't it?" Kevin asked, putting her arm around my shoulders. "Asa's almost ready to start school. Thanks to you, he'll be able to go to the same school I did."

"Lots of people made that happen," I said, "but I'm glad he doesn't have to ride a bus to another town."

"First the school," Kevin said. "Now, downtown. I have a hard time keeping up with you."

"You're the one who buys houses by the dozen," I said.

"Yes, but all this." Kevin gestured at the collection of students working through a list of chores Luke had drawn up.

When she moved her hand, I saw it. A giant—and I mean giant—diamond solitaire glistened on Kevin's left hand.

Torn between taking her hand to gawk at the ring, hugging her, and screaming with delight, I did a combination of all three. "You're engaged!" I shrieked. "When? How? That ring is stunning. When's the wedding?" I enveloped her in a bear hug and whirled her around, her elegant hair working loose.

"You're making me dizzy," she said. "We're trying to keep it low-key."

"Low-key? This is a big deal."

"You don't think it's too soon?" Her face was solemn. "With Daddy gone and Mama hurt . . ."

"No way, Kevin! Marcus is smiling down from heaven," I said, trying not to cry. "Your mom must be ecstatic."

"We told her last night," Kevin said. "She said this is what she and Daddy wanted more than anything for me and Asa." A sweet expression came to her face as she looked over at

Terrence. "After all that's happened, we didn't want to wait any longer. I hope people don't think it means I don't miss Daddy."

"People understand," I said. "Everyone will think that you've finally come to your senses."

"You and my mother sound just alike," Kevin said.

Tammy scurried over to check out what was going on, starting a parade of people. "Is that an engagement ring?" she screamed. "I'll take your wedding pictures if you want." Then she wiggled her eyebrows and lowered her voice. "I can also give you tips on being married to a lawyer."

"Isn't it strange how life turns out?" Katy asked, as she and Molly hurried over to check out what was going on.

Terrence walked back from checking on Asa, and his smile gave me chills. "So you decided to tell our good news?" he said.

"Lois pried it out of me," Kevin said.

"What kind of friend would miss a rock like that?" I asked.

"Without you, Lois, I might never have gotten Kevin to give me a second look." Terrence put his arm around Kevin's waist. "She kept saying she didn't have time for me, but you wouldn't let her get away with that."

Chris joined the group, congratulating the couple. "I hope this doesn't mean you and Asa are moving to Alexandria," he said.

I held my breath.

"Leave Green? Never!" Kevin said. "Terrence and I are officially buying Major's development. We'll hire someone to run it and the Lakeside Motel."

"You're buying Major's property?" Tammy let loose with a belly laugh. "That is priceless. He wouldn't sell you one house and now you'll own the entire subdivision."

"Not much he can say since it's practically in foreclosure," Terrence said. "His attention seems to be on staying out of jail.

Mossy Bend is the least of his concerns from what I hear down in Alexandria."

My eye caught Chris's and Tammy's, but I didn't ask the dozen questions I had. This moment wasn't about the ugliness of Major.

"Will you move into one of the lake houses?" Tammy asked.

"Nope," Kevin said. "We're staying right where we are."

Terrence pulled Kevin even closer. "Our family wants to do its part for Green," he said. "We plan to be here a long time."

Kevin couldn't shake her wedding nerves, which Tammy tried to joke her out of.

"Your feet are so cold, your ice sculpture should be shaped like shoes," Tammy said while taking the formal wedding portrait.

"Tammy . . ." I said.

"Don't start, Lois," Tammy said. "That dress is gorgeous, and I want to make sure Kevin gets a chance to wear it."

Kevin adjusted her hem. "I'm trying," she said.

"You love Terrence, and he loves you." I attempted a calm, Iris Jo tone.

The bride-to-be fingered the antique lace on the gown, custom-made for her by my crankiest advertiser. "I don't know," she said. "It doesn't seem right."

"Her hair looks great," Tammy said, moving in for a close-up shot. "The curls around your face are a nice touch, Doc."

I shooed Tammy out the door under the pretense of getting hair spray out of Kevin's car.

"We want it to stay that way," I said, trying not to grit my teeth. "Why don't you get the hair spray while Kevin and I talk about the wedding?"

"Oh, hair spray," Tammy said, when I threw her a not-very-subtle look. "I'm on the case."

As she left the room, Kevin started to sit down, and I yanked her arm. "Not in your dress," I wailed. "You'll wrinkle it."

"I can't get married," she said and reached for the tiny fabric-covered buttons on her back. "I've just decided. Mama needs me. Asa and I have made it as a family this long. I'm not doing it."

"Does the groom have any say in this?" I chose my words carefully.

"Terrence will understand," she said. "He knows things have changed since . . . since that day." Moving around behind her to help with the buttons, I eased her out of the dress. I didn't say anything, which was becoming something of an unexpected habit.

Kevin looked at me with the sorrow she'd worn for the past few weeks. "I can't get married without Daddy there. And Mama might not be well enough either . . . Why did I rush this?" Tears made her eyes glow. "It's not the right time. Maybe next year, when Asa's older and things aren't so up in the air."

I sat next to her and fingered the skirt of the dress that hung nearby. "Perhaps this is the perfect time to get married," I said in a voice so gentle it surprised me. "You can take what you learned from Pearl and Marcus and use it to shape your own family."

"I'm afraid," she said.

"I know."

"I hate it, feeling afraid. It's not me, but I can't get rid of it. What if something happens to Terrence or Asa? How will I live with that?"

"I don't know," I said. "Maybe you'll all live to be a hundred, but if not . . . You'll get through it. Somehow we get through the bad times."

She looked over at the gown and smoothed her hair. "Terrence will be a good husband, won't he?"

I felt the beginning of a smile inside me. "He most certainly will."

"And he'll make Asa a good father."

"Without question," I said.

"Do you think we could elope?"

"I suppose you could," I said, "but you'd disappoint a lot of people. I was looking forward to being your matron of honor. I like the dress Barbara made for me."

Kevin smiled tremulously. "I wonder if Tammy's found the hair spray yet?"

The Taylor family church, small and old-fashioned, overflowed on the evening the town's first African American doctor and her strong lawyer fiancé tied the knot, little Asa standing next to the man who would become his adopted father.

The day had been all steamy Louisiana late-August, but the bride looked cool and serene, bright green shoes peeking out from under the hem of her traditional gown. The small, family ceremony had ballooned into a big wedding, put together in record time.

"It's time," I said in the foyer, as I listened for my cue from the organ. "You ready to do this?"

"More than ready," she said, giving me a careful hug before I opened the door. "How's Mama?"

"She's settled up front," I said. "She's just waiting for her baby to walk down that aisle."

"Lois, I wouldn't have made it without you," Kevin said. "Thank you." She kissed my cheek, and I squeezed her hand and walked into the sanctuary, glowing with dozens of candles. Making my way forward, I saw members of the Lakeside Neighborhood Association, who had benefited from the Taylors' fight for civil rights, neighbors from the street that Kevin had renovated for affordable housing, and movers and shakers, including Mayor Eva and Dub, a judge or two, and several state politicians.

Chris, handsome in a rare suit and tie, turned as I entered and smiled when I passed the aisle where he sat, giving a quick thumbs-up.

Asa, bouncing from foot to foot next to Terrence, fidgeted with the bowtie on his miniature tuxedo and gave me a big grin before saying, "Hi, Miss Lois," in a stage whisper.

When the first chords of the Wedding March sounded, Terrence reached down and took Asa's hand. The doors at the back opened, and Kevin entered carrying a bouquet of pink roses, her mother's favorite flower.

With careful, even steps, she walked up the aisle alone, stopping to hand her mother, in a wheelchair near the aisle, one of the roses. Kevin then placed one on the empty seat on the front left of the sanctuary, bowing her head and closing her eyes for a brief moment.

When she looked up, she smiled at Terrence and Asa. They stepped forward to take her by the hand.

"Wasn't that the most beautiful wedding?" Katy gushed as we gathered at the country club for the reception. "I thought I was going to lose it when she walked down the aisle."

"She's gorgeous," Molly said, monitoring Asa, who was drawing at the children's table.

"You don't look so bad yourself, Lois," Katy said, turning to me. "Miss Barbara's getting good with her designer gowns."

"She's already taking orders for Mardi Gras balls all over the state," Tammy said, shooting a photograph of Molly and Katy before putting the camera on a nearby table. "Since that picture of Lois's wedding dress was in that magazine, she says her business has been fabulous."

"Barbara is an example of how a business can flourish in a small town," I said, patting my sleek gown.

"Did she make yours, too?" Molly asked Tammy, who wore a slinky, vivid yellow dress with geometric white and black squares. A gold chain with an aquamarine stone replaced her usual chunky beads.

"I got this dress in Shreveport," she said.

"And that necklace?" I asked.

"Walt bought this in Dallas when we went over to celebrate . . ." her voice disappeared. If she hadn't been Tammy, I might have thought she blushed.

"Did Walt win another big case?" I teased.

Tammy fingered the stone and looked across the room where her husband was talking to Chris, who was holding Eddie.

Her hand rested on her stomach.

"This is the birthstone for March," she said in the quietest voice I had ever heard her use. "We're going to have a baby."

"Were you scared?" Tammy asked when she came into my office with Monday's mail.

Perplexed, I frowned. "Scared? Of what?"

"Were you scared when you found out you were pregnant?"

"Oh, yes," *I'd say so.* "You know I like to be in control, and having Eddie was all new."

"I'm terrified," she said, pacing around the office. "I'm afraid to tell people in case something goes wrong."

I moved to the front of my desk and patted the chair next to me, the way I usually did for Katy and Molly. "Everything's going to be fine."

"What if I'm a terrible mother?" she asked, ignoring the chair and leaning against my desk. "It's not like I had the best role model."

"You'll be a great mom," I said. "And Walt will make a fantastic father."

"He will, won't he?" she said with the softer look she wore when discussing her husband. "He's already bought three baby books, but I expect most of my pointers to come from you and Iris."

I thought of that very morning when Eddie had managed to dirty not only his diaper but the cute sheets in his crib and then had spit up on my shirt after I'd gotten dressed for work. I'd left the house nearly in tears, Chris trying to calm both of us and offering to drop Eddie off at his mother's.

Then I recalled the night before when I'd gone in to check on Eddie, and he was making baby-sleep noises and smiling what Chris called his "chasing puppies" smile. I had stood there so long watching him that Chris had come in to see if something was wrong.

"Being a mom is the hardest—and easiest—thing you'll ever do," I said to Tammy.

Tammy had gone out to her desk, and I was analyzing the newspaper's budget numbers when the phone rang.

"Lois, it's Becca," a hysterical voice said when I picked it up. "Cassie's sick, and I don't know what to do. She won't stop throwing up, and her fever keeps getting higher and higher. I can't reach Lee, and I couldn't think of anyone else to call."

"Where are you?" I asked.

"At the shop," she said, "Can you drive me to Shreveport? My mother can't leave my brother."

"I'll be right there."

Explaining to Tammy on the run, I jumped in my SUV and drove the short distance, double-parking in front of the shop. Saying a prayer for the little girl, I tried to remember what I'd learned from Kevin about dehydration and children's viruses.

Kevin! Of course! Maybe we could reach her and not have to risk the trip to Shreveport.

"We're back here," Becca called when I entered the shop.

Past the curtain in the workroom, Becca held Cassie in her lap and stroked her forehead with a wet towel. The girl's cheeks were flushed, and she was listless, not giving me her usual cheerful grin.

"If you can drive us, I can sit in the back with her," Becca said, standing without putting the child down. "We can go to the ER at LSU Hospital."

"I have a better idea." I headed for the phone. "I'll call Kevin and see if she can see Cass at the clinic. She and Terrence and Asa just got back from their trip, and I talked to her last night," I jabbered as I dialed. "She should be in this morning."

"I don't know," Becca said with a hesitant gulp, looking from Cassie to the phone and back. "We can get to Shreveport in less than an hour."

"But Kevin's right here."

"What if she doesn't want to help us?" Becca asked.

"Kevin is a doctor," I said. "Nothing comes between her and sick children."

"I don't know if I have the nerve to face her," Becca said and then looked at the child in her arms, smoothing Cassie's damp curls. "Go ahead and call her. Please. Hurry."

A pediatric nurse let us in the back door of the clinic and showed us to a small examination room with a Noah's Ark mural painted on the wall. "Dr. Kevin will be right with you," she said, murmuring encouraging words as she took the fretful girl's temperature and recorded her list of symptoms.

Kevin whooshed into the room in her lab coat, the scent of soap and antiseptic accompanying her, going straight to Cassie, who now lay on the exam table.

"So we're not feeling so hot today, huh?" she asked in the same tone she used with Asa. "We're going to get you all fixed up." She picked up her stethoscope and listened to the girl's heart, explaining everything she did in the words of a relaxed kindergarten teacher.

"Cassie, you have a good heart," Kevin said, smiling as she moved the instrument from the girl's chest.

Cassie gave a puny smile, and Kevin looked at Becca with compassion. "How long has she been vomiting?"

"Since the middle of the night," Becca said. "She stopped for a little while this morning. I thought she had a stomach bug, and I brought her to work with me." She looked apologetic. "I hated to leave her with my mother when she felt so bad."

While they spoke, Kevin looked in Cassie's throat and ears with a light, and moved her arms and legs up and down.

"It hurts when she walks, too," Becca said. "She couldn't even make it to the bathroom on her own."

"It's probably a bad virus," Kevin said, "but we'll run tests to make sure." Her calm professionalism lowered my anxiety, and I could tell it helped Becca, too.

"Let's take some pictures of your bones, how about it?" Kevin said to Cassie and stuck her head out of the door to call for a nurse's help.

"Why don't you and Lois come along while we get X-rays?" Kevin said. "We need to do blood work, too."

Returning to the exam room after the lab work, Kevin made a big show of taking Cassie for a ride in a wheelchair. "She's got a serious virus, and you may have a few more rough days," Kevin said. "I'd like to see her again in about three days. If she gets worse, bring her in sooner. But she should be much better in a couple of days."

"Oh, thank heavens!" Becca said, grabbing Cassie's cheeks and kissing her forehead.

"Try not to worry," Kevin said, heading for the door. "Everything is going to be fine."

"Thank you, Doctor," Becca said, reaching out to touch the lab coat.

As Kevin vanished, Becca looked at me. "She has a good heart, too," she said.

18

My neighbor Trish McGuire asked me to spread the word that she is not taking any more volunteer jobs this year. "I just wore myself out with the fund-raiser for the arts center. I promised Randy I wouldn't take on anything else until I went on a few fishing trips with him. Our community needs more people to lend a hand. Think about where you might be needed."

—*The Green News-Item*

The instant Pastor Jean took the microphone I knew today was the day.

My heart gave a little flip, and my eyes watered.

Jean's husband, Don, sat on the front row and gave her a smile, and she mirrored that smile as she looked out into the congregation.

"Jesus used a handful to spread God's message," she said as she wrapped up her sermon. "He asked ordinary people to follow him, and they did."

A couple of older men said "amen," and I waited.

"Christ asks us again today to follow him," she said. "Right now. Whoever we are. Whatever we're doing." Chris reached for my hand. "I find myself called to a new place. I ask you to carry on God's work at Grace Chapel with the joy and faithfulness you have always shown."

"Oh, no," someone said, and the pianist bumped against the keyboard, making a jarring chord. Murmurs moved through the room as people commented on her announcement.

"What did she say?" the oldest member asked.

"She's leaving," his wife whispered so loudly that our entire side of the church could hear.

The man made a snorting sound. "Never did like having a woman preacher, anyway."

After the benediction, members rushed to Jean's side, but I hung back.

"I'll get Eddie," Chris said, brushing his hands against my hair the way he did when I was troubled.

I watched him head to the nursery, and then moved closer to the clog of members around Jean. People had crowded around Jesus in the same way, I thought, and I imagined the members of Grace in dusty robes and sandals, crying out for mercy. Somehow it wasn't very hard to picture.

"You're a mighty fine preacher," my father-in-law said to Jean, and I thought of what a perfect disciple he would have been in those early days.

"The best," Estelle said, hugging Jean, and I could see her welcoming the band of believers into her home for a meal.

"I'll never forget the funerals you preached," a tiny elderly woman in a church dress said.

"Or the way you helped us build this new church," another said.

Jean's husband had taken a seat near the back of the church, and I walked over to him. "She's changed us all for the better," I said, my voice quivering.

Don nodded. "This has been a very difficult decision."

I smiled. "God has something else for her to do, and she's ready to take it on."

"I never planned to marry a preacher," he said, "but I guess God's call isn't always what we expect, is it?"

"That's for sure," I said and walked over to where Chris and Eddie had entered.

Thank you, God, for calling Jean to us in the first place.

Giving up my Sunday afternoon reading, I drove to the parsonage with a bouquet of roses from the yard.

Don was loading the car for his drive back to Baton Rouge, and I wandered around Jean's living room while they said their farewells, looking out the front window to see Jean waving until his car disappeared from sight.

"I won't miss doing that," Jean said as she entered the carport door.

I turned, teary-eyed again. "How have you done it for so long?" I asked. "I couldn't stand to be away from Chris like that."

The preacher gave an almost self-conscious shrug. "I thought Don would move to Green when I got my assignment to Grace Chapel. The longer he stayed away, the easier it got to say goodbye."

Nodding, I wasn't sure I understood.

"Don and I have realized it's not good for us to be apart," she said, "and he's not willing to quit his job. So, I'm going back to Baton Rouge. It's what God is nudging me to do."

"But you're leaving without another job," I pressed. "I don't get it."

Settling into her prayer chair, where she had contemplated many decisions, she waited until I was situated on the couch.

"I'm doing what I told you to do all those months ago," she said. "I'm waiting. And trusting."

She quirked her lips into a very un-Jean-like shape. "We'll see if I'm able to take my own advice."

"God is already preparing the people on your path," I said.

"Lois, are you sure you're not a preacher?" she asked. Shadows that had been on her face since our conversation weeks earlier had lifted.

"No way." I threw a pillow at her, and she laughed. "You mentioned the transition this morning, but not a date. What are you thinking?"

"I'll be here a few more weeks," she said. "If the congregation chooses Luke, I'll move sooner."

"But he's so young," I said. "The older members might tear him to pieces."

"It's not the older members I'm concerned about," she said. "They've taken him under their wings. The ones your age are the ones who might think he's not quite seasoned enough."

I considered that. "He's like a cross between a big puppy and the cute teacher everyone wanted in high school. I don't know if he's ready to lead his own church."

"He'd bring the energy and zest that Grace needs," she said, "but whatever happens, as you've pointed out, God will go before us."

Both Chris and his mother were chosen to be on the pastor-search committee and, at the congregation's urging, expanded the search, choosing three area preachers to listen to.

The duo had gone to a tiny church north of Shreveport to hear a sermon, and Hugh had come to our house after church to wait. I'd fed Eddie, put him down for a nap, and then assembled a Sunday lunch that, though not up to my mother-in-law's quality, was considerably better than I'd made before marrying Chris.

Walking in with the day's eggs, four tiny Bantam ones, he held them up as though he'd laid them himself. "I left two on the nest," Hugh said. "Figured Eddie might enjoy watching them hatch."

I turned back to the cake mix I was stirring and grinned. "Eddie or you?" I asked.

"Both," he said.

The dogs yelped their familiar welcome as Chris and Estelle pulled into the driveway.

"How was it?" I asked before they were barely out of the truck.

"I don't think that fellow was one bit better than Luke," Estelle said.

Chris agreed. "He's more mature than Luke, if gray hair counts, but his preaching was a little . . ."

"Dull!" his mother said. "Go ahead and say it. His preaching was dull. There were two or three people around us who fell sound asleep."

"The room was a little warm," Chris said. "I'm not sure the air-conditioner was working."

Hugh said the blessing as we prepared to eat. Estelle raved about my roast beef and then grew more serious. "Lois, what do you think Grace needs in a preacher?"

A few years ago the question would have seemed preposterous, but the little church had become a cornerstone in my life. "I'm not sure who it should be, but I know it's time to let Jean go," I said.

Chris's fork stopped halfway to his mouth. "You've been so sad about her leaving," he said. "I figured you'd want to keep her around as long as possible."

"I used to feel that way," I said, "but I realized that Jean's only part of what makes Grace special." I passed Hugh a bowl of green beans with almond slivers, and refilled tea glasses as I talked. "Maybe we could ask Luke to stay as our interim pastor and see how it goes."

"I suggested the same thing to the committee on the way home." Estelle almost cackled, she was so pleased. "We can give him six months to a year and see how he does."

Pastor Luke, as I was attempting to call him, came to our house a few nights later to talk about his new role. I scarcely recognized him when I opened the door.

"Do I look like a preacher?" he asked with his familiar grin when I gasped at his short hair and his ironed shirt and slacks.

"Well, you don't look like Pastor Jean," I said, "or Pastor Mali at the Methodist church, but I guess you'll do."

Chris, Luke, and I sat on the back porch, the ceiling fan stirring up a faint breeze. Eddie chattered on the floor in between chewing on a rubber toy that Holly Beth kept trying to grab.

"Sorry," I apologized as I moved the dog away from the baby for the dozenth time and tried to pacify Eddie, who wanted to grab Holly's fur. In the yard, the three bigger dogs barked for attention. "It's always a zoo around here."

"I like your place," Luke said, moving down to the floor to play with the baby. "I look forward to having a family some day . . . if I live through my first preaching job."

"You're doing well," Chris said, his legs spread out and his hands behind his head, "but what's with the haircut?"

Luke looked embarrassed. "A few people mentioned that my hair was too long. I decided if it bothered them that much, I would get it cut."

The conversation meandered through the evening, the frogs and crickets nearly drowning out Luke's deep voice from time to time as he talked about moving into the parsonage.

"I never imagined myself settling in a place like Green," he said. "I don't mean settling, like it's not my first choice. I mean settling like putting down roots."

"It's got to be quite different from where you went to college," I said.

"You know how it is, Lois," he said. "You moved here from a city up North."

"The Midwest," I corrected. "Dayton, Ohio."

"Roots are good," Chris said. "You never know who's going to move down the road from you." He threw me one of his looks that made my heart beat faster. "Lois showed up and swept me right off my feet."

"You swept me off my feet, too," I said. "That's what happens, Luke. Someone will show up for you."

"Watch out, Pastor," Chris said, "you're in the presence of a world-class matchmaker."

The young preacher looked uncomfortable. "Some of the older members told me it's not a good idea for the pastor to date. They said people can take it the wrong way, like the hair and jeans."

"They'll change their story as soon as they have a granddaughter they want you to meet," Chris said with a laugh. "If there's anything a group of church people can't stand, it's a single man."

We laughed together.

"And don't worry about the jeans," I called to Luke as he got in his Jeep. "You have to give them something to fret about."

When Chris and I tucked Eddie in a few minutes later, I thought of Luke. "I must be getting old," I said, turning on the soft nightlight. "I feel like Luke has grown up before my very eyes."

"I was just thinking the same thing," Chris said.

Jean protested at the idea of a going-away reception, but the church, me included, would not hear of canceling it.

"You have to give people the chance to say goodbye," I scolded. "You can't possibly leave without a party."

"I don't think I'm up to preaching a farewell sermon," she said. "It seems too final, and I don't want to cry in front of everyone."

"What if Luke preaches?" I asked. "Could you handle that?"

"That'd be perfect," she said. "I'll do the children's sermon and ask him to do the rest."

Jean invited parents to bring all their children, even the babies, into worship. The pianist played a medley of hymns while we gathered at the front with Jean and Luke for what the older members called children's church. The pastors each carried a medium-sized cardboard box.

Iris Jo and I sat on the floor with Ellie, Eddie, and the rest of Grace's growing collection of children, including Maria's boys, who'd been such an integral part of Jean's ministry.

"Good morning," Jean said, and then added, "Buenos dias." Kneeling, she reached into one of the boxes and pulled out a children's Bible, a picture of Christ on the cover. "The word of God tells us that we must become as children to enter the kingdom of heaven. Looking at you amazing youngsters, it's easy to understand why Jesus said that."

She extended her arms, and gestured. Several of the children moved closer. "Pastor Luke and I bought you a present," she whispered. The children's eyes widened, and they edged closer. "My favorite book in the whole world."

I knew the money for the Bibles had come from Jean's own pocket, and my heart filled as I watched her and Luke hand them out, Jean calling each child by name. "Eleanor Lois and Edward Thomas," she said as she came to us, reaching over to kiss each baby before she handed us their Bibles. "Train them well," she murmured.

As we delivered the babies to the nursery, Molly sang Jean's favorite hymn, "It is Well with My Soul," a last solo before Molly and her family moved. A tide of contentment and sadness washed over me as the music floated through the air.

"I hate goodbyes," I whispered to Chris, who slipped his arm around me and pulled me close.

Luke, who had filled in a handful of times for Jean, cleared his throat when he walked to the lectern to preach. "Uh," he said. "Uh."

I held my breath.

"Uh," he said once more. Then he looked out at us and grinned, a big, boyish smile. "I'm unbelievably nervous."

The congregation laughed and seemed to relax at his confession.

"Maybe we should pray again," he said, and another chuckle accompanied the rustle of people bowing their heads.

"Lord, you know and I know that I can't do this all by myself." His deep voice was a sharp contrast to Jean's. "I come to you and ask you to use me to speak to these, your people."

Stillness fell over the room at the power of his words, and Luke jumped into his message with the determination of a baseball player running for home plate. "The Bible is filled with young people who were asked to serve," Luke said. "Samuel. David. Joseph. Esther. And that's only a start."

"Amen," a person or two said.

"Pastor Jean has been a blessing," he said, "and I ask you to pray for God to guide her and me as we do our best to bear fruit that lasts."

"You've got it," one man shouted.

"We're already praying," another man said.

"What'd he say?" the elderly man said loudly.

Both Jean and Luke smiled broadly, and I knew I had watched the future unfold in more ways than one during that service.

19

The Novel Theology Book Club is holding its Cover-to-Cover Cupcake Sale to raise money for books for children. Flavors include chocolate (of course!), wedding cake, and red velvet, the best-seller each year. The club would love for you to read along with them and consider ordering cupcakes, which come in batches of a dozen.

—The Green News-Item

The pharmacy owner suggested a parade.

The hardware store owner wanted a farmers' market.

"Perhaps we could have another festival," the Baptist minister said.

Most people agreed we should unveil the painted fish a few at a time, starting with an event.

At every suggestion, banker Jerry shook his head so hard he looked like one of those dolls with a spring for a neck. "We've tried those in one form or another," he said, "and they didn't work."

"I suggest we have the streets re-striped for a bicycle lane," one of Green's newer residents said. "It will encourage people to ride their bikes downtown."

A hum of "no way" swept around the room.

"The last time I rode a bicycle I was ten years old," Jerry said. "A special lane isn't going to get me back on two wheels, and it won't bring money downtown. We need an industrial park to offset the losses. Who knows when we'll get our lake back?"

The conference room grew quiet at his comment, and two or three people turned to look at Zach, who had come to the meeting with Jerry.

I had promised Zach that the *Item* would experiment with Post Media on one big project, in return for his help getting the sculptures in place. He was still living in the Lakeside Motel but had not opened a local office. Several businesspeople greeted him by name, while a handful of others looked at him suspiciously.

"I'm intrigued by the effort you have put into revitalizing Green in the last few years," he said. "Post is happy to be part of the public art project."

"You know I appreciate your company's interest in our town, Zach," Jerry said, "but that catfish thing is about the silliest darned idea I ever heard. They may do that kind of thing in big cities where they have money to burn, but we need to invest in practical things here."

Zach's response was identical to what it had been years ago in Dayton news meetings. He nodded, made a small clicking noise with his mouth, and said nothing.

"I disagree, Jerry," Eva, whose interest in the idea had escalated in the last couple of weeks, said. "Lois delivered a fresh idea when we needed one."

Wearing a stylish vest and a pressed Oxford shirt with the sleeves rolled up, she only needed a cigar to look like an old-timey politician sealing a backroom deal. Her painted fingernails and large ring kept the image from going any further, however.

"That decision has been made," Rose, who had taken a day off from her mail route, said. "We need to think of our next step."

"None of these suggestions is likely to draw a crowd downtown," Jerry said. "We barely broke even with the Ice Cream Social, and that's been Green's biggest event for four years."

"Not to mention the amount of time it takes to put these kinds of events together," the head of the town's biggest civic club said. "We work months on those."

"We don't have months," Iris said. "Revenues reflect the number of cars you'll see outside at lunch time." She moved her thumb and index finger in a shrinking gesture.

Zach looked at her with interest. *Oh, no, fellow, you're not getting my office manager.*

"The same with antiques," Rose said. "The Holey Moley has made half what it had at this time last year. Without drastic improvements, we'll be forced to close."

"Downtown is having a ripple effect on the other businesses," Jerry said. "We need leadership."

Trying to stop another campaign speech, I interrupted. "What we need is momentum. We're stalled."

"We're not stalled," Jerry said. "We're downright finished."

The air of gloom in the room was as thick as the heat and humidity outside.

"We are not finished," I insisted. "Green isn't like other towns."

"Not every little town dies," Dub, who had taken a renewed interest in downtown, said. "There are many charming towns around the country, and they have vibrant downtowns."

Jerry all but thumped his chest. "You saw what the support was for those ideas Becca brought back from that highfaluting meeting. Towns are about suburbs, not Main Street."

"Jerry's right," an auto-parts storeowner said. "The time for downtown retail has passed. That happened years ago."

Becca squared her shoulders. "So we're prepared to give up?"

"If I've said it once, I've said it a hundred times," Jerry said. "People aren't interested in downtown anymore."

I drew in my breath, certain that I'd been present for every one of Jerry's hundred pronouncements on the future of Green. "The way some of you talk, we might as well have a giant garage sale and call it quits," I said. "If we'd acted like this, we'd never have recovered from the tornado or kept the school open."

"That's our answer!" Becca said, jumping up.

Nearly everyone in the room, including me, threw her quizzical looks, but she didn't seem to notice. "What if we tried a giant garage sale? Lots of places are doing that."

Her idea was about as well-received as another tornado. The meeting immediately disintegrated into a collection of individual conversations, filled with "no" and "can't." As the chairman of the group, I tried to get everyone's attention and finally pounded my fist on the table.

"One at a time," I said.

Zach gave me a surprising nod of approval.

"I don't see how getting people to clean out their closets is going to save downtown," the pharmacy owner said.

"Do we really want to be known as the town that sells junk?" Jerry said.

"It might be better than being the town that no one ever heard of," Rose said.

I turned to Eva. Although she looked doubtful, she never ruled an idea out without thinking about it. "It would be relatively inexpensive," she said.

"And not take much time to plan," Iris added.

"Those of us with downtown businesses could have sidewalk sales," Rose said.

"We can make it a big deal, and that will bring people to Green," Becca said, exhibiting more enthusiasm than she had since her grandmother's collision.

"It might help the neighborhoods closest to downtown, like Lakeside," Pastor Mali said.

Tammy, who had stepped in to take photographs of the meeting and, I suspected, grab a box lunch, spoke. "People line up before daylight for garage sales in our neighborhood."

"My band could play at the park that night," said a local real-estate agent. "We do oldies, and we're pretty good."

The energy level in the room rose faster than Chris's ponds after a hard rain.

"Post Media might be willing to underwrite such an endeavor," Zach said, looking at me. "This is the kind of community-building the grant wanted to fund. Would the *Item* work with us?"

"That's possible," I said, hating to share another project with him, but knowing it was imperative if I hoped to gain a consensus.

"It'd help to have a big-name company like that," Jerry said, although it was clear he hadn't yet decided to agree. "How much will you contribute?"

"I'll have to check with our marketing department," Zach said, "but I'm sure it will be substantial."

"We'll vouch for the idea and write a check today," I said. "I can work with Zach to swap advertising."

"I move that we try a downtown garage sale with *The Green News-Item* and Post Media as corporate sponsors," the hardware store owner said.

The collection of business owners, civic leaders, and pastors split right down the middle on the vote. Mayor Eva, the most un-garage-sale person I'd ever met, broke the tie.

"One last thing," Becca said as the disgruntled members began to disperse. "Do we need someone to direct traffic?"

"Now, Becca," Eva said, "That's what I call optimism."

"To direct this town to bankruptcy court," Jerry said with a very good imitation of one of Major Wilson's harrumphs and stormed out.

Within two weeks, the event that Tammy called Downtown CPR had mushroomed into Green's Labor Day Garage Sale Extravaganza. The Bayou Freez would reopen that Saturday afternoon, and a band would play on the lakefront that evening.

Zach stopped by the paper before the big weekend, preparing to return to his corporate offices in Omaha.

"You're leaving?" I asked. "But tomorrow's the big day. You've put a lot of time and money into this."

"That kid Alex who used to work for you is going to run our office here," he said. He sank into one of the chairs across from my desk, Holly Beth running over and chewing on his leather wingtips. "Alex can maintain our presence and dig up that Major Wilson story for our regional papers. We will beat you on that story."

Although I'd hoped he would leave, it made me feel weirdly defensive. "You didn't give Green a chance," I said. "This is a great place to do business."

"That's not what you've been telling me the past six months," he said. "You know corporate expects quick returns. We're not giving up, but we'll look for ways to do this more efficiently." I decided not to remind him that efficiency was what had brought him to Louisiana in the first place.

"What do you have on Major?" I tried to keep my face impassive. Linda had almost enough for us to go to press and for Major to go back to jail. I didn't intend to be beaten on this one, no matter how Zach's ego disagreed.

"Lois, we might have worked together on community projects," he said, "but you're not going to pry a news story out of me. How about you? What do you have?"

I looked him straight in the eye. "You'd better get a mail subscription to the *News-Item*."

"I'll do that," he said.

Tapping my desk, he picked up the photograph of Eddie that Chris had given me for our anniversary. "At least Green helped get me transferred back home. Being down here made me realize that whatever I do, it has to be closer to my boys."

He picked up a paper clip and twisted it, and I had a strange feeling of déjà vu. "I don't know if I'll ever put down roots like you have, though."

We'd had a similar conversation the day of Ed's funeral in the Dayton newsroom. My sadness that day had made me wonder if anything would ever be right again. *Wow. How life had turned out.* "You'll figure out the right thing," I said. "I've found it helps to pray about it."

Nodding with a tiny smile, he got up and headed to the door, turning before he disappeared into the lobby. "Didn't your nickname used to be Scoop?" he asked.

"Ed called me that." I smiled at the memory.

"Good luck with the ice-cream business, Scoop," he said, then saluted and left.

Promising free ice cream and a sneak peek at one of the catfish sculptures, I invited the planning committee, of which I had wound up as chair, to a final meeting at the Freez that afternoon before the event.

A ripple of nerves jumped in my stomach as I started down Main Street toward Bayou Lake with Iris Jo. Carrying a three-ring binder bulging with notes and permits for food vendors, who promised everything from fried pickles to roast beef sundaes, I had an anxiety attack.

"This was a bad idea," I said. "No one holds a garage sale to save a town. Especially not the weekend they open a new business they know nothing about."

"Quit worrying," Iris said, holding up a stack of that afternoon's paper, four pages bigger than our usual Friday run. It included a complete guide to the yard sales, a downtown flea market where vendors had rented stalls, and an art sale in the park, most accompanied by advertising. "At least we're not sitting around doing nothing like some little towns."

"What if no one comes?"

"Look around," she said.

Pulling myself away from my anxiety, I noticed businesses putting up decorations for the next day and four or five cars driving down the street, a few other vehicles parked in front of the Holey Moley and Eva's store.

"Lois, Iris, wait up," Becca called, almost running to catch up with us.

"You're certainly chipper," Iris said, and I liked the way the word sounded.

"We're having a great day at the shop," she said. "I've even had to call in my helper for the first time in ages. I've sold more today than I have in the last month."

"This might actually work," I said.

"Two of my customers are staying at the motel out south so they can hit the garage sales bright and early," Becca added. "Your publicity worked."

"At last tally, it was in five daily newspapers, television stations in Shreveport and Alexandria, and in a magazine in Shreveport and Bossier," Iris said and smiled when I turned to stare at her. "I made a log to keep track."

"And it was on page one of *The Green News-Item*," Becca said, pointing to Katy's giant headline that read, "Say Hello to Downtown with Good Buys: From Flowers to Furniture, A Day of Fun Awaits."

My spirits lifted as they talked.

"Not to mention all the coverage we're getting on the art project," Becca said. "And entries from all over the country. What a fantastic idea that was."

After staying up too late to make sure all the details were in order, I was exhausted the next morning. "You go on without me," I moaned to Chris when the alarm went off before daylight. "I think I'll sleep in."

"I tried to tell you this was too much on the weekend we open," he said, poking me in the ribs in a way that should have been annoying but instead was endearing. "Why are you always the one who has to save the planet?"

"You were right." I pulled the cover over my face, muffling the words.

"What did you say?" he asked. "I didn't quite catch that."

Eddie's wake-up jabber sounded on the baby monitor, and I stuck my head out from under the cover with a smile.

"Duty calls," I said. "We've got to get our son dressed for his first garage sale and grand opening."

With Eddie in tow, Chris and I parked at the Bayou Freez, Main Street blocked with flea market booths and food stands, the smell of funnel cakes already hanging in the air, a thundercloud hanging over town.

"Nothing like hot grease on a September morning," Chris said. Sweat dripped off both of us as we took a last look around the drive-in.

"See you for blastoff," I said, kissing him and holding tight for a moment.

Iris Jo and I had agreed to set up camp at the paper for the morning, directing news coverage and attempting to solve whatever crises a day of bargain hunters might bring. Chris and Stan would troubleshoot at the Bayou Freez until we opened in late afternoon.

We put Eddie and Ellie on a pallet in my office, where they seemed content enough for the moment.

"It's hard to believe that Labor Day weekend means the end of summer in some places," Tammy said, pulling her hair up off her neck as she came in, her stomach not yet bulging under her oversized orange T-shirt.

"Only two months of hot weather left," Walt said, standing behind her.

"It's good to see you today," I said. "I thought you might be tired of the Freez by now."

"Miss the Green cultural gala of the year?" he said and moved in to give Iris and me a hug. "I can't wait to see the first of those catfish sculptures."

If it had been anyone but Walt, I would have suspected he was poking fun at me, but I knew he was sincere.

"They're worth the wait," I said with a smile.

"It's raining," Katy said, dashing in from the parking lot. She had come home for the long weekend after only three days back at school, full of excitement about the semester ahead. Ahhh, Katy.

"This weather's supposed to blow right over," Stan said.

Debating whether to be thankful it wasn't a tornado or agitated because the town would be soggy, I looked at Eddie and Ellie playing on my office floor and decided on gratitude. "We've done all we can," I said.

Linda came in from the newsroom, a smile on her face, before Katy had managed to comb the raindrops from her hair. "The police radio reports traffic jams all over town," the reporter said. "All over town. They're calling it Garage Sale Madness."

I looked at Iris, who intercepted my request without any words. "Go on," she said. "I'll keep an eye on Eddie."

Katy and I set off down Main Street under a steady drizzle, steam rising from the pavement. The vendors had swathed their tents in plastic, creating an overall effect of being in a terrarium, but no one seemed all that bent out of shape.

"I guess they're used to it," I said, as we watched middle-aged women with backpacks haggle over the price of old china and clocks that didn't work.

"They do have cool retro stuff," Katy said. "I had a doll like that when I was a kid."

"You still are a kid," I said with a smile. "Let's see how Becca's doing."

The rain stopped by the time we reached the florist's shop, and Lee Hicks and Cassie were rearranging merchandise on a table outside. Lee's shirt was damp, though it was impossible to tell if it was from the rain or the heat, and Cassie, recovered from her virus, was beaming.

"Looks good," I said, my heart happy to see the father and daughter together.

"My helper here did it all," Lee said, resting his hand on her curls.

"I'm working," Cassie said before giving me a big hug around my knees. "With my daddy."

It took all of my resolve not to cry, and Lee seemed to be having the same problem. "Becca's inside," he said. "She's making corsages or something."

Two or three shoppers browsed inside. Becca held up a basket of single daisies with a loop of yellow ribbon and a pin. "Welcome back, Katy! May I offer you a flower, ladies?" One of the blossoms was stuck on a clip in her hair.

"But of course," I said, letting her pin one on my blouse.

"Me, too, me, too," Katy said.

She and Becca had become friends since the Vince ordeal."She told me she made stupid mistakes when she was my age, but everything worked out," Katy had said. "I like hanging out with her."

Looking at them today, I was fascinated by how life had brought them together.

"Are we still on for the concert tonight?" Becca asked.

"For sure," Katy said. "Luke didn't have anything to do, so I told him he could come too, if that's OK."

"Cassie loves Brother Luke," Becca said.

"Don't we all?" I said. "If some women would come to their senses . . ."

Katy groaned. "You know Chris doesn't like it when you play matchmaker."

"Maybe not," I said, "but even Chris thinks Luke could be the perfect man for you."

"I keep telling you we're just friends," Katy said. "I don't want another long-distance relationship. Besides, I'm not marrying a preacher." She drifted out the front door and Becca chuckled.

Checking with her customers, Becca walked back to the window, where I watched the busy scene outside. "How about you and Lee, Becca?" I asked softly. "He sure seems to spend a lot of time around here."

"We're . . . What did Katy call it earlier? Oh, yeah, just friends." Looking down at the flowers in her hand, she snipped a stem. "Lois, I'm not sure I want to get mixed up with him again."

"But you are mixed up with him." I looked at where Cassie stood near Lee.

"We're trying to work all that out," Becca said, "and I've tried to be understanding. But that doesn't mean there's anything more for us."

Lee lifted his T-shirt to wipe the sweat from his face, and Becca sighed. "He is a nice-looking man, though."

"Why don't you give him another chance?" I said.

"Fear. Plain and simple. Fear," she said. "What if he hasn't changed?"

"I know he has," I said, watching him kneel down to speak to his daughter.

Becca's mouth curved into a tender smile. "We'll see," she said.

20

A free dental clinic for horses will be held at the parish fairgrounds next Wednesday. All properly vaccinated horses are welcome to come by for a checkup. "The Bouef Parish Livestock Management Office is committed to keeping local animals healthy, from hoof to mouth," Dr. Finn Truett said.

—The Green News-Item

Whose idea was it to open a drive-in restaurant?" Chris asked with a smile when Eddie and I entered the kitchen that Saturday afternoon.

"You can kill me later," I said.

"Pulling out all the stops, are we?" he said. "Giving me that earnest, hopeful look. You know I can't resist that."

My face might be the color of Becca's geraniums, but I loved it when Chris flirted and teased. What a blessing to have a husband who could make a day like today feel fun.

Stretching to give him a peck on the lips, I pointed to the line of traffic on the street in front and the people milling around on Main Street to the side. "You really should kill me. I hope we can handle everyone."

Chris leaned over and tweaked my nose. "We've served half the town ice cream these past few weeks," he said. "Joe and Maria can run the machines in their sleep."

Maria, who had wiped the counters more times than I had counted the cones, smiled. "You help people," she said. "People will remember that when you open tonight."

"All will be well, Miss Lois," Joe said.

"Will your boys be able to come," I asked, "now that Pastor Jean's gone?"

"Dub and Mayor Eva are bringing them," she said.

Joe's weathered face crinkled as he smiled. "Tonight we will have a true celebration."

"Thank you," I said, noticing that both Joe and Maria had added a trace of Louisiana to their Spanish accents.

I tugged on Chris's T-shirt sleeve. "Let's check outside one last time."

"The rest of the supplies need sorting," he said, looking through my planning notebook. He pointed through the window. "Katy and Luke have the sidewalks swept, and Becca told Lee how to start decorating the tables. We're on kitchen duty with Joe and Maria."

I inclined my head in Chris's trademark "let's get out of here" look, the one he gave me when I visited too long after church or stayed too long at a wedding. "Let's check it out," I said.

Stepping into the hot September afternoon, I nodded back to where Joe and Maria shared a hug and quick kiss before turning back to their chores. "I thought so!" I said.

Chris looked through the sparkling glass. "Can't you give it up for one day?" His voice sounded incredulous, but he had the teasing glint in his eye.

"They make a great couple," I said and held up my fingers to count. "Maria and Joe. Iris and Stan. Tammy and Walt.

Kevin and Terrence. Me and you." I frowned. "If we could only get Eva and Dub . . ."

"Lois . . ." he interrupted with a warning note in his voice. "You're pushing your luck. Let's go back over our checklist."

The temperature was bearable, which in early September in Louisiana meant it had stopped short of the century mark. The faintest hint of a breeze blew from Bayou Lake. Only a few pockets of water were evident, and the weeds were tan. It looked more like a Kansas plain than a Louisiana lake. Biologists predicted it would take an extreme winter and more research to eradicate the plant.

In late afternoon, the sun was high enough in the sky to cast a bright glow on the old building, which oozed charm. The hand-lettered menu board boasted two dozen flavors of milk shakes, and perennial favorites like hot fudge sundaes and banana splits. Becca had put red-checkered plastic tablecloths on the tables and anchored them with wildflower bouquets in old soft-drink bottles.

An excited buzz circulated through the outdoor space as neighbors visited, catching up on topics ranging from whether Eddie weighed more than Ellie to how good tomatoes were this year. Pearl Taylor's arrival in her wheelchair, with Asa on her lap, brought elated hellos and gentle hugs.

Watching Chris greet Pearl with Eddie cradled in his uninjured arm, I was flooded by contentment with our decision to buy the Bayou Freez. Maybe it would be a magnet to draw people downtown.

Pearl's voice shook when she spoke to me. "I am so proud of you, Lois. You have made Green the kind of place Marcus and I always dreamed it could be."

I wiped my eyes and kissed her paper-thin cheek. "I'm so thankful to be here," I said.

As more people gathered around Pearl, Chris, Eddie, and I walked away, Chris ruffling my hair and then our son's. "You were right about us buying the Freez," he said.

"Thanks for going along with me," I said, putting my arms around his neck.

"Shouldn't you two be working?" Tammy said, making me jump.

"Quit lurking," I said as she snapped a picture of me, Chris, and Eddie.

"Everyone in town is showing up." Tammy pointed to Bud and Anna Grace, the agriculture columnist and his wife, our food correspondent. "You've managed to get the youngest citizens of Green here with the oldest, the mayor and every other mover-and-shaker in the parish."

"What a marvelous turnout, Lois," Eva gushed. Wearing white linen Capri slacks and a bright red silk T, she had the broad smile of an election-night victory. "I haven't seen this many people downtown in years."

"I didn't know there was such a call for soft-serve ice cream," Dub said.

"Your investment made the difference," I said.

"We'll sell it to you," Chris said.

"At a profit," I joked.

"I might just think about that," Dub said. He looked over at Joe Sepulvado, who was straightening extra chairs, and grinned. "This is a wonderful new beginning for downtown."

"And to think that rotten brother of mine wanted to tear it down," Eva said.

"I nearly punched him when he told me he planned to tear this down and build an industrial park," Dub said. "I knew it would break your heart."

"So that's what your fight was about," Katy said, walking up in a pair of cutoff jean shorts and a Bayou Freez T-shirt. "Molly and I saw you arguing."

Eva jerked her head slightly, her perfect bobbed hair swooshing with the motion.

"I didn't want him to hurt you anymore," Dub said quickly.

"I've taken care of myself for years," Eva said.

"I want to take care of you from now on," he said softly, and I felt as though they were continuing a conversation that had started earlier. "Please do me the honor."

"Oh, my gosh," Tammy gasped. "Did you just propose to her?"

"Yes, I did," Dub said. He took both of Eva's hands in his. "Eva, will you be my wife? I can stay home and help run the Bayou Freez while you take care of Congress."

In the background, people laughed and talked, and music blared from the speakers attached to the front of the building. But the huddle around Eva and Dub was as quiet as a library.

Eva looked at Dub with a stunned expression. She did not, however, withdraw her hands from his grasp, nor step back. No one else moved either.

"Don't turn me down again," Dub said. "What better place is there to accept than here?"

Eva's bottom lip quivered almost imperceptibly, and tears came to her eyes. "This is where we had our first date," she said.

"And where I first told you I loved you," Dub said.

Tammy had stopped snapping pictures, and Katy's mouth formed an "O."

Dub pulled out his ever-present white handkerchief and dabbed the corner of each of Eva's eyes. "I fell in love with you forty years ago, and I've never stopped loving you."

"I love you, too," Eva said. "It'd be my great pleasure to marry you."

They moved together to kiss, and I squeezed Chris's hand. "Yes!" I said. "Our first engagement at the Bayou Freez."

The circle around us erupted in applause and cheers. Luke, looking like a seasoned pastor, glanced up from kissing a baby and headed our way. He moved through the crowd, hugging older women and shaking hands with the men. Sweat sparkled on his brow when he drew near Chris and me.

"Now that we have Eva and Dub taken care of, we need to start," I said. "Pastor Luke, will you say a few words?"

"Uhh." He wiped his forehead on the sleeve of his University of Texas T-shirt. He seemed to have as many college T-shirts as Pastor Jean had souvenir sweatshirts.

"Don't sweat it, Luke," Chris said with the smile I so loved. "People are here for ice cream. Anything you say will be lagniappe."

Luke looked confused. "They didn't teach me that word in seminary."

"Lagniappe," I said. "A little something extra."

"Oh," he said.

Katy, with Molly, also in town for the weekend, had set up a small table for her T-shirts, which were selling as fast as I hoped peach shakes would be shortly. A large bouquet of free red and white helium-filled balloons floated near the table, children approaching in swarms to get theirs.

"Come on, Lois," Katy called. "What's the holdup?"

"We're convincing Luke to say the blessing," I said.

Katy threw the pastor an encouraging smile. "You'll do great," she said. "And they'll pay you in ice cream."

"If I mess up, will you pop a balloon to distract the crowd?"

"Absolutely," she said. "I'll be right up front."

We waded to the front of the building, generous Green hugs and congratulatory compliments flying through the air.

"Coach and Lois have, uh, asked me to say a few words on the reopening of the Bayou Freez," Luke said, tearing the bottom off a milkshake cup to make a megaphone.

"We are blessed to get together to hang out like this. I, uh," He looked up, his words shifting, confident now. "We preachers can't let a crowd gather without a sermon. And this looks like the feeding of the five thousand."

The crowd gave a laughing groan.

"You have taught me much about welcoming strangers," Luke continued. "In only a few months, you've shown me what it looks like to love one another."

The crowd quieted, apparently charmed by his earnest words, this handsome young preacher, this old-fashioned dairy bar. As Luke bowed his head, others followed, one by one, some clasping the hand of the next person.

"Our God, may this place touch lives in gentle and generous ways," Luke said. "Bless this town as it seeks your guidance, that whatever it does will be done in love. May we serve you by serving others."

For a split second, there was a holy moment.

"Time to unveil the catfish," Katy yelled to laughter and cheers, the moment gone, the emotion lingering.

Anna Grace and Bud, chosen to do the honors, moved to the corner near the Bayou Freez. "Voilà!" Anna Grace said as she yanked the sheet away. Painted by a local senior citizens' art class, the giant fish pictured Main Street the way it had looked a hundred years earlier. Bayou Lake was bright blue in the background.

I hoped it would look like that again. The sun shone down on the fish. Cameras flashed and citizens jockeyed for their turn to be photographed next to it.

Eva borrowed Luke's makeshift megaphone and reminded the audience that more sculptures would go up in the next few months. "And, now," she said, "as a gift from my future husband and me, free ice cream!"

Joe lifted the two serving windows and turned around the plastic "open" sign, bought at the Dollar Barn, south of town. "May I help you?" he asked, and our first line formed, Tammy recording all of it with her camera.

By dusk, the mosquitoes were out and the unofficial numbers were in. Swarms of card-carrying antiquers and junk lovers had invaded Green, spilling over into cafes and stores and eating an amazing number of corn dogs and roasted peanuts.

Sitting outside the Bayou Freez, a small group of us watched people gather in the lakefront park, spreading quilts and blankets and setting up folding chairs. Maria and Joe had strung old Christmas lights around the front of the ice-cream stand, and they twinkled in the evening, the line steady at the counter.

"The idea to have live music was a good one," Iris said, handing Ellie a cracker to chew on. "I'm even getting used to the lake looking like a field." Eddie sat on the quilt next to the little girl, the usual jabbering coming from his mouth.

"Have you noticed that Eddie takes after his mother when it comes to talking?" Chris said.

"That thought has crossed my mind," Stan said as he and Chris headed up to the window.

Ellie and Eddie watched the two men intently. Then, Ellie grabbed the concrete bench, pulled herself up, swayed a time or two, and took a step.

"She's walking!" I said to Iris. "She's walking! Look at your girl go."

At the sound of my excitement, Eddie looked at me, looked back at Ellie for a second, pulled himself up on the bench, and plopped back down, a startled expression on his chubby face. He flopped over on the soft quilt, labored up on his hands and knees like a turtle, and rocked a time or two.

With a happy smile, he crawled over to Ellie.

Iris and I looked at each other and laughed.

Chris and Stan walked up with milkshakes as I dashed a tear out of my eye, something I seemed prone to lately.

"Did we miss something?" Chris asked.

"Only two more Green milestones," I said. "That's the future of Green right there. They'll make all of this better." I waved my arm at the scene before us and took my shake from Chris's hand.

"What flavor did you get me?" Iris asked.

"That weird pistachio one you've been craving," Stan said.

"That's the same flavor Lois wanted," Chris said with a quizzical look.

I smiled. "I'm glad I stayed in Green," I whispered to Chris.

"I am, too," he said.

Discussion Questions

1. In *Downtown Green*, Lois and the town encounter problems faced by real-life towns. What are some of these? Have you observed any similar issues in towns where you or your family have lived? What can small towns do to stay vibrant and inviting?
2. Lois is struck by how quickly life changes. What are some of the changes she experiences? What do you think is hardest for her to deal with? What advice would you give Lois as she continues to develop? How do you handle change in your life?
3. At one point in her busy life, Lois makes up headlines about her days. If you wrote headlines about your life, what would they say?
4. Lois and Chris are learning to lean on each other. In what ways do you think Chris changes Lois? In what ways does she change him? What sort of family life do they have? Have you ever wished for a different family routine? What changes might you make to enjoy your family more?
5. Katy and Molly grow as young adults and find that life is a series of choices. Do you agree with the choices they make? In what ways are they still like the high-school girls they were when Lois met them? How have they matured? What might you suggest to Lois to help her mentor these two young women? What did Katy learn from her online dating experience?
6. Pastor Jean is one of the people Lois has depended on during her life in Green, and Jean has leaned on Lois through the years. Why do you think Jean makes the decision she does in *Downtown Green*? Do you agree with her? Why or why not? Have you ever faced a time when you felt that God was calling you in a different direction than you expected? How did you handle it?

7. Luke is a newcomer on Route Two, as Lois once was. How would you describe his entry into Green life? What do you think about his role at Grace Community Chapel? Have you ever watched a church change as people come and go? What ideas do you have on how to make transitions easier?
8. Lois and Chris continue to redo their old home to make a cozy nest. What does the home represent to Lois? If you were describing their home, how would you describe it? How would you describe your dream home? What characteristics would you want it to have?
9. Becca, the young florist, tries to run her business and has issues to deal with. What are some of the problems she faces? How would you describe her character? What might Lois learn from her? What might she learn from Lois? Have you ever tried to help someone with his or her life? What did you learn from that experience?
10. Characters such as Lee Roy Hicks and Zach appear in ongoing Green stories, each of them intersecting with Lois. Why does it bother Lois that her former boss shows up in her current life? What do you think of Lee Roy Hicks's efforts to right his wrongs? Do you believe these two men are sincere?
11. The Bayou Freez Drive-In reenters Green in this story. Why is this business important? Do you recall a similar spot from your younger life? What was it like?
12. Mayor Eva finds politics draining and must defend herself against charges of wrongdoing. Was she unfairly accused? What do you notice about local politics where you live?
13. What do you think of Dub's part in this book? What has he learned from his earlier years? What will the future hold for him and Eva?

14. Lois is on a journey where she believes everything works out for the best. In what ways is this proven true in her life? Do you believe things will work out well in your life? What steps might you take to enjoy each day more?

Want to learn more about author
Judy Christie and check out other great fiction
from Abingdon Press?

Sign up for our fiction newsletter at
www.AbingdonPress.com
to read interviews with your favorite authors, find tips for starting a reading group, and stay posted on what new titles are on the horizon. It's a place to connect with other fiction readers or post a comment about this book.

Be sure to visit Judy online!

www.judychristie.com